Lisa tilted her head at a sassy angle and said, "I know it's hard to imagine, but I haven't always been this shy and sweet."

Wyatt grinned wickedly. "You're right. I do find that hard to believe."

He glanced down to where her coat had fallen open, giving him his first up-close glimpse of her legs. His reaction was eager and as predictable as nightfall. By the time he managed to drag his gaze back to her face, she was staring at him knowingly.

She covered her legs and cast him a look that spoke volumes. When she finally did say something, it was in a soft, conciliatory tone of voice he didn't like one bit. "I hope you don't take offense, Sheriff, but I'm afraid you're just not my type."

Dear Reader,

Welcome to another wonderful month at Silhouette Romance. In the midst of these hot summer days, why not treat yourself (come on, you know you deserve it) by relaxing in the shade with these romantically satisfying love stories.

What's a millionaire bachelor posing as a working-class guy to do after he agrees to baby-sit his cranky infant niece? Run straight into the arms of a very beautiful pediatrician who desperately wants a family of her own, of course! Don't miss this delightful addition to our BUNDLES OF JOY series with *Baby Business* by Laura Anthony.

The ever-enchanting award-winning author Sandra Steffen is back with the second installment of her enthralling BACHELOR GULCH miniseries. This time it's the local sheriff who's got to lasso his lady love in *Wyatt's Most Wanted Wife*.

And there are plenty of more great romances to be found this month. Moyra Tarling brings you an emotionally compelling marriage-of-convenience story with *Marry In Haste*. A gal from the wrong side of the tracks is reunited with the sexy fire fighter she'd once won at a bachelor auction (imagine the interesting stories they'll have to tell) in Cara Colter's *Husband In Red*. RITA Award-winning author Elizabeth Sites is back with a terrific Western love story centering around a legendary wedding gown in *The Rainbow Bride*. And when best friends marry for the sake of a child, they find out that real love can follow, in *Marriage Is Just the Beginning* by Betty Jane Sanders.

So curl up with an always-compelling Silhouette Romance novel and a refreshing glass of lemonade, and enjoy the summer!

Melissa Senate
Senior Editor
Silhouette Romance

Please address questions and book requests to:
Silhouette Reader Service
U.S.: 3010 Walden Ave., P.O. Box 1325, Buffalo, NY 14269
Canadian: P.O. Box 609, Fort Erie, Ont. L2A 5X3

WYATT'S MOST WANTED WIFE

Sandra Steffen

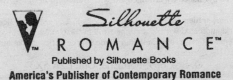

Silhouette

ROMANCE™

Published by Silhouette Books

America's Publisher of Contemporary Romance

For my friend Betty Dikeman, who inspires me,
encourages me, teaches me, accepts me, ponders life
with me, humbles me and laughs with me.

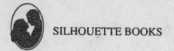 SILHOUETTE BOOKS

ISBN 0-373-19241-X

WYATT'S MOST WANTED WIFE

Copyright © 1997 by Sandra E. Steffen

This edition published by arrangement with Harlequin Books S.A.

® and TM are trademarks of Harlequin Books S.A., used under license.
Trademarks indicated with ® are registered in the United States Patent
and Trademark Office, the Canadian Trade Marks Office and in other
countries.

Printed in U.S.A.

SANDRA STEFFEN

Creating memorable characters is one of Sandra's favorite aspects of writing. She's always been a romantic, and is thrilled to be able to spend her days doing what she loves—bringing her characters to life on her computer screen.

Sandra grew up in Michigan, the fourth of ten children, all of whom have taken the old adage "Go forth and multiply" quite literally. Add to this her husband, who is her real-life hero, their four school-age sons who keep their lives in constant motion, their gigantic cat, Percy, and her wonderful friends, in-laws and neighbors, and what do you get? Chaos, of course, but also a wonderful sense of belonging she wouldn't trade for the world.

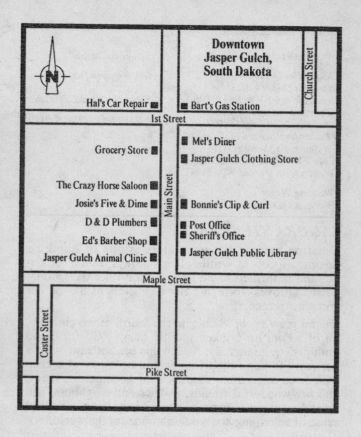

Downtown Jasper Gulch, South Dakota

Church Street

Hal's Car Repair

Bart's Gas Station

1st Street

Grocery Store

Mel's Diner

Jasper Gulch Clothing Store

Main Street

The Crazy Horse Saloon

Josie's Five & Dime

Bonnie's Clip & Curl

D & D Plumbers

Post Office

Sheriff's Office

Ed's Barber Shop

Jasper Gulch Animal Clinic

Jasper Gulch Public Library

Maple Street

Custer Street

Pike Street

Chapter One

Sheriff Wyatt McCully pulled the brim of his white Stetson lower on his forehead and peered into the far corners of the crowded old diner. He wasn't sure how the ordinary Tuesday town meeting had turned into a party. One minute he'd been sitting in the back room with the other members of the town council, groaning along with everyone else as Isabell Pruitt, the leader of the Ladies Aid Society self-righteously rose to her feet. For months the old prude had been spouting that ill would come of the ad the local boys had placed in the papers to lure women to their corner of South Dakota, and tonight had been no exception. Just when Wyatt thought Isabell would never run out of wind, someone had called to adjourn and a party had broken out.

Normally he enjoyed the small-town crowd. But tonight he would have preferred a more private setting.

Leaning back in his chair, he stretched his legs out underneath the small table and crossed his arms. Voices rose, and laughter echoed from one end of the diner to the other. The bachelors of Jasper Gulch were noisier and bawdier than usual. He figured they had good reason to be cheerful.

Yesterday's rain had put an end to the worst drought in twenty-two years. Luke Carson's engagement had ended a similar dry spell among the Jasper Gents. Wyatt was happy enough about both of those things, but they didn't account for the sense of urgency driving him to distraction tonight.

Laughter, deep and rich and feminine, drew his gaze. The crowd parted, awarding him a clear view of the woman who was responsible for the rousing pull at his insides. It obliterated every coherent thought in his head, but it came as no surprise. It had been pulsing like a blip of radar ever since Lisa Markman had set foot in town a month ago.

The woman had a flirty walk, an infectious grin and a wink that could stop a hundred-and-seventy-five-pound man in his tracks. Wyatt was normally the most patient man in the county, but his patience was wearing thin. He was getting mighty tired of sitting back while every bachelor in Jasper Gulch vied for her affections. Push had come to shove. It was time for Wyatt McCully to make his move.

He stood and surveyed the room. Steadily making his way around the small groups of people blocking his path, he gave a brief nod now and then. But most of his attention was trained on the woman he intended to meet.

Lisa's back was to him, and although he had to admit he preferred a woman who was walking toward him, he couldn't find fault with the way she looked from behind. There wasn't another woman in town with hair as dark as hers. There wasn't another woman in town who could make a simple pair of jeans and a red Western shirt look like something straight out of a man's fantasies, either. It was probably just as well that the noise drowned out the rasp of his deeply drawn breath, but he doubted there was anything that could have chased away the anticipation lengthening his stride.

"Look, Opal, it's Wyatt McCully."

"Why, yes, Isabell, yes, it is."

Wyatt jerked to a stop, barely managing to keep from running headlong into the two gray-haired women who'd planted themselves directly in his path. With a grudging tip of his head, he said, "Evening, ladies."

"Why, isn't he just the most polite young man, Opal?"

"Yes, Isabell, I do believe he is. I was just saying as much to my Louetta a few minutes ago."

Wyatt shifted to the right and his attention strayed, his eyes automatically picking Lisa out of the crowd. Not that it was difficult. With the blip of radar steadily working its way lower in his body, he could have found her in the dark.

"Have you had a chance to talk to Louetta lately, Wyatt? She's sitting at that table right over there."

He cast a perfunctory glance at Opal Graham's daughter who waved shyly then proceeded to blush three shades of red. He hadn't actually spoken to Louetta lately. Back in high school, the boys had voted her The Girl Most Likely Not To.

"She's a lovely girl, don't you think?" Isabell asked.

Louetta? Lovely? The *girl* was thirty-three years old. If she had any curves, they were hidden underneath high necklines and baggy clothes. Wyatt had no idea why Isabell was singing her praises to *him*, but when Lisa's throaty laughter carried to his ears again, he didn't stay long enough to find out. Ignoring Isabell's affronted huff, he plowed his way to the front of the room.

He was only six steps away when he noticed the coffee carafe in Lisa's right hand, only two steps away when she finished filling his grandfather's cup and gave him a gentle nudge. "Cletus McCully, you must have been a real lady-killer in your day."

"Who says my day is over?"

"Why, Cletus, are you flirting with me?"

"I see I ain't losin' my touch."

Laughing, Lisa eased away from the table. Wyatt might

not have appreciated his grandfather's flirting, but he'd have to be out of his mind not to enjoy the gentle brush of Lisa's hip against his thigh. His hands automatically went to her waist, and for one brief moment her gaze swung to his. Her laughter drained away, leaving behind the most amazing half smile.

Lisa Markman swallowed. Hard. She'd been in South Dakota a month, but this was the first time she'd gotten an up-close-and-personal look at Wyatt McCully's lean face. The fact that she'd been keeping her distance hadn't exactly been a coincidence. She'd noticed him watching her now and then, and she knew what his look did to her. She wasn't a snob, but she wasn't stupid, either. She'd come to this town that had advertised for women, because it seemed like the perfect place to start over, to find a man to love, someone like her—a little outspoken, a little beaten up by life. The local sheriff with his sterling badge and reputation to match simply wasn't the man for her. It was too bad, too. She'd come across a lot of men in her day, but she hadn't met many as appealing to her as the tall, lean, fair-haired Wyatt McCully.

A primitive warning sounded in her ears, bringing her to her senses. She couldn't have been more relieved when Bonnie Trumble, who owned the Clip & Curl down the street, signaled for more coffee at a table a few feet away. Lisa filled the empty cup and topped off another.

"You're very good at that."

She turned slowly. Facing Wyatt, she told herself he was referring to her coffee-pouring abilities. He hadn't said or done anything to make her think he'd meant something else by his simple words of praise. In all fairness it wasn't his fault her imagination had given his statement another meaning. It was his voice. No man should be allowed to own such a voice, let alone use it as if it was meant for her ears alone.

Trying to put an end to the awareness arcing between

them, she motioned to the crowd. "Although I'm only helping your sister tonight, I've done more waitressing than I care to think about. Believe me, I have the fallen arches to prove it."

If she could have called back her words, she would have. Maybe then his gaze wouldn't have taken the slow route to her feet, resting on forbidden places along the way. Maybe then she wouldn't have been so aware of the swooping pull on her insides. But she was aware, and when the light touched upon Wyatt's white cowboy hat, she knew she had to put an end to it, here and now.

She stepped to one side and made a show of glancing around. "I'd better get busy. That sister of yours cracks a mean whip."

His forward motion was sure and easy, and so was his smile. Both sent her thoughts into a tailspin.

"You must know that Mel's bark is worse than her bite. This party's going to break up any minute. I just heard some of the boys talking about moving it over to the Crazy Horse. What do you say we duck out the back door and drive into Pierre for dinner?"

"Dinner?"

He smiled again, and danged if her gaze didn't get stuck on his mouth. There was a long pause during which she fought for self-control. Her mind cleared gradually, and her determination returned. If there was one thing her life had given her, it was plenty of practice handling touchy situations. Giving him a wink she'd perfected years ago, she said, "Thanks, Sheriff, but I don't think that would be a very good idea. Now, if you'll excuse me, it looks as if Melody and Jillian want to talk to me about something."

Without another word, she ducked into the crowd, making a beeline for the front of the room. Wyatt clamped his mouth shut and watched her go.

He hadn't realized he wasn't alone until Cletus's crotchety voice cut into his thoughts. "So, things didn't quite come off without a hitch, eh, boy?"

With Lisa's reply sitting on his ego like a box of rocks, Wyatt shot his grandfather a penetrating look. "Whatever gives you that idea?"

Cletus hooked his thumbs through his suspenders and slowly shook his head. "It could have something to do with the fact that you look like a stallion with a sore—"

Wyatt heard Isabell's and Opal's dramatic gasps, so he wasn't surprised when Cletus said, "Hoof," instead of what he'd probably intended to say. "Well?" his grandfather asked, turning his back on the two eavesdroppers and lowering his voice. "Did you ask her?"

"I asked her."

"And?"

"She turned me down."

Cletus snapped his suspenders and shook his head. "Jumpin' catfish, she ain't makin' it easy on ya, that's for sure."

Wyatt didn't reply. Cletus had raised him, and if there was one thing he was used to, it was his grandfather's huge understatements. Besides, Cletus was right. Lisa wasn't making it easy on him. In fact, she was making it next to impossible.

A spoon jangled on a glass, drawing everyone's attention to the front of the room where Lisa and her best friend were standing. "Can I have your attention, please?" Lisa called.

At least twenty people said, "Shh." Twenty more yelled, "Quiet," but it took a two-fingered whistle from Wyatt's sister, Mel, to silence everyone enough for Lisa to be heard.

"Before Luke whisks Jillian out of here tonight—to make wedding plans, of course—I'd like to propose a toast."

The room echoed with resounding chuckles from the

local bachelors. Everybody knew Luke Carson, and nobody believed for a minute that he had wedding plans on his mind tonight. Luke was Wyatt's best friend. Judging from the glowing expression on Jillian's face, he was also a lucky man. Wyatt had a sudden, burning desire to arrest somebody. If there wasn't a law against that kind of happiness, there ought to be.

Raising her pot of coffee, Lisa said, "To Luke and Jillian, the first couple to become engaged in Jasper Gulch in more than five years."

One of the local boys shouted, "The first but not the last."

"I'm plannin' on being next," someone else called.

"Right after me."

"In your dreams."

"If I'm dreaming these days, it ain't about you."

When the ensuing argument died down, Jillian Daniels pushed her wavy red hair behind her shoulders and raised her own glass. "I'd like to propose a toast, too. To Lisa Markman, the best sport in the world. After all, it was her idea to move to a town that advertised for women, her idea to actively search for Mr. Right. She's systematically dated every man who's asked her, yet, like the true friend she is, she's genuinely happy for Luke and me."

Hearty chuckles and guffaws nearly raised the roof. Wyatt glanced at Lisa, and he couldn't join in. His heart beat a steady rhythm that had nothing to do with laughter. Just when he was convinced she wasn't going to look his way, her gaze met his. She went perfectly still, and so did he. Awareness flickered in her eyes, sending a flush to Wyatt's face and chest that had nothing to do with the August temperatures. Something incredible made its way through him. Before he could put a name to it, Luke's brother, Clayt, said something to Jillian and Lisa, and the moment broke.

Tipping his hat back with one finger, Clayt raised his

voice so that it could be heard from one end of the diner to the other. "I just want to remind everybody to keep the first Saturday in September open. The town council is hosting a barbecue in Luke and Jillian's honor, and everyone's invited."

Jillian beamed, and Lisa didn't look at Wyatt again. He knew, because he watched her for a long time. Wondering if he could have been mistaken about what he thought had passed between them, he finally turned away. Nursing a sore ego, he headed for his quiet corner in the back of the room.

"Lisa, are you okay?"

Lisa peered through wispy bangs that were on the verge of being too long, and found Jillian Daniels watching her closely from the other side of the breakfast table. "Why wouldn't I be okay?"

Seemingly lost in thought, Jillian rose to her feet and carried her cereal bowl to the sink. "I don't know," she said after she turned the water off and placed the bowl upside down in the drainer. "Maybe it has something to do with the fact that you've sighed three times in the past five minutes."

"I have not."

"Yes, you have."

"Jillian, I couldn't possibly have sighed three times in the past five minutes."

"Maybe you're right."

Lisa started to smile, thinking this was more like it.

"Maybe it was four times."

Shaking her head, Lisa carried her own cereal bowl to the sink. When she glanced at her friend again, Jillian was leaning against the counter, in the house they'd shared since moving from Wisconsin earlier in the summer. Jillian's arms were crossed, her gaze unwavering. It was a stance Lisa knew well. Jillian Daniels had long red hair, soft blue eyes and a stubborn streak a mile wide. Although she rarely admitted it out loud, it was one of the things Lisa had always been the most thankful for. Without it, Jillian never would have been able to talk her into going to live with Ivy Pennington all those years ago, and Lisa might never have stopped running.

"Are you going to tell me what's bothering you?" Jillian asked in a quiet voice.

Tucking a wayward strand of hair behind her ear, Lisa shifted her weight to one hip and said, "Does Luke know how persistent you can be?"

"Believe me, he knows. Luke is so incredible. *Love* is so incredible. No wonder you wanted to move out here and experience this."

"Yes, well, you're just lucky you're my best friend. Otherwise, I'd be mad at you for nabbing the most eligible bachelor in Jasper Gulch."

"Are you mad at me?"

"Pu-lease."

"Then my engagement to Luke doesn't have anything to do with those sighs of yours and the fact that you were so quiet last night and again this morning?"

The reason for Lisa's quietude and her sighs shimmered across her mind. She didn't want to think about Wyatt McCully, but she couldn't seem to get the expression deep in his eyes and the clear-cut lines in his face out of her head.

She glanced at her friend and found Jillian watching her closely. She'd been on the receiving end of Jillian's treasured smiles a thousand times, which was just about how many whispered secrets they'd shared over the years. Their friendship went back a long time, through petty misunderstandings, life-altering heartaches and far-reaching dreams. Lisa knew she could tell Jillian anything. She even knew that Jillian would probably say that whatever had taken place between her and Wyatt last night had been fate. Lisa might have believed in fate, but she certainly didn't rely on it. Determination was ten times more powerful, and Lisa was determined to put Wyatt McCully out of her mind, once and for all. It shouldn't be too difficult. Of the sixty-two bachelors in Jasper Gulch, there were still forty-nine she hadn't dated. As far as she could tell, only one of them wore a white cowboy hat and had a reputation just as pure. That left forty-eight men to choose from and only one to steer clear of.

"Well?"

Her friend's voice drew Lisa from her thoughts. Jillian looked as if she was waiting for an answer, which would have been okay if Lisa could have remembered the question. Ducking her head slightly, she said, "What were we talking about again?"

Jillian spun around. "I knew it. You *are* upset about my engagement to Luke."

Lisa rolled her eyes and shook her head. "Tell me you don't really believe I have a thing for your fiancé."

"You did go out with him."

"Only because *you* insisted. I already told you we talked about *you* all evening," Lisa said, remembering the date she'd gone on with Luke Carson a few weeks ago. The man had been attractive and funny and so deeply in love with Jillian they really hadn't talked about much else.

"Then you really don't have strong feelings for Luke?" Jillian asked slowly.

"Of course not. Now would you please go start the car so we can both get to work?"

Jillian looked at her for several seconds. Seemingly satisfied that Lisa was telling the truth, she reached for her purse and hurried into the living room.

"Jillian?"

The other woman stopped at the front door and turned around, "What?" written all over her face.

"Would you give Luke up if I asked you to?"

Jillian had the grace to pretend to think about it before letting loose a smile bright enough to light up the room. "Not on your life, sister."

Lisa laughed and Jillian grinned then slipped through the screen door. Feeling better than she had all morning, Lisa checked the stove, grabbed her purse and raincoat, and followed. She was in the process of pulling the front door shut behind her when Jillian's voice rang out from several feet away.

"Where did you park the car last night?"

Lisa walked forward, down the steps and across the sidewalk. She didn't stop until she reached the exact spot in the driveway where she'd left her car the previous night. Except for a few shallow puddles, the driveway was empty. "I parked it right here where I always do."

"That's what I thought. It's gone. Somebody must have taken it."

Lisa turned in a circle. "I'll be danged."

"What are you doing to do?" Jillian asked.

Gauging the clouds hanging low in the sky, Lisa said, "I'm not sure, but if my new clothing store is going to be a success, I need my car to pick up the new fall merchandise in Pierre this afternoon. For now, it looks like we're walking to work."

Spinning around, she went inside for an umbrella.

"Oooo-eee. It's really coming down out there."

Wyatt glanced up in time to see Luke Carson close the door behind him and shake the water from his black Stetson. With a jauntiness one rarely associated with a Carson, he called, "Hey, Wyatt, do you have any more of that coffee?"

Wyatt scribbled something on a notepad, then shoved the traffic ticket he'd issued last night into a folder, wondering when his office had turned into one of those coffeehouses they had in the city. Oblivious to his friend's

dark mood, Luke whisked a chair away from the wall and
straddled it. Crossing his arms along the top, he grinned
inanely at nobody in particular.

Wyatt glanced at the other Carson brother, who was
slouched in stony silence in the chair next to the desk.
Meeting Wyatt's gaze, Clayt shook his head and spoke for
the first time in fifteen minutes. "He's been like this ever
since Jillian agreed to marry him two days ago."

"Been like what?" Luke asked with entirely too much
wonder in his voice.

Clayt didn't have to speak. The sardonic lift of his eyebrows and the tilt of his head said it all.

Wyatt pushed his chair away from his desk and strode
to the filing cabinet, where he sloshed coffee into three
cups, wondering what it would take to get a little privacy
around here. People claimed misery loved company, but
he would have preferred to sulk alone. That was next to
impossible in Jasper Gulch. He should know. He'd tried it
last night. He really had had every intention of nursing his
sore ego in his own quiet corner in the diner. But when
he'd gotten back to his table, his corner hadn't been quiet
anymore. He'd taken one look at the area ranchers and
cowboys he'd grown up with and had hightailed it over to
the Crazy Horse Saloon. Glancing at the two men taking
up space in his small office right now, he realized he
wasn't having much better luck this morning.

"Ah," Luke said, after taking his first sip of coffee.
"Thick as tar. Just the way I like it."

Clayt slunk lower in his chair and shook his head all
over again. Wyatt almost grinned for the first time since
yesterday.

Luke and Clayt Carson were a year apart in age and
shared a passing family resemblance that included dark
hair, gray eyes and tanned skin pulled taut over high
cheekbones and angular chins. Their tall, lanky builds had

come from the same gene pool, but the good mood Luke was in today didn't run in the family.

Wyatt knew both of these men like the backs of his hands. He'd been there when Clayt had gotten married ten years ago. He'd been there when his wife had left him two years later, too. Wyatt was the first person Luke had told about his decision to become a vet instead of a partner on the family ranch. Technically, only Luke and Clayt were blood related, but Wyatt had been in and out of the Carson house so often while he was growing up he might as well have been a third brother, blond hair, brown eyes and all.

"So," Luke said cheerfully. "What's new?"

Clayt slanted Wyatt a meaningful look. "I liked him a lot better when he was ornery, didn't you?"

Luke laughed. "Come on, you two. I'm going to marry the most beautiful woman in Jasper Gulch. You should be happy for me. Who knows, maybe one of you will get lucky one of these days."

The outer door opened noisily. Before Wyatt and Clayt had the opportunity to *offer* to wipe the grin off Luke's face, Cletus McCully closed the door and ambled closer.

Staring at the water running off his grandfather's hat and the footprints on the floor, Wyatt said, "Granddad, you're dripping wet. Where have you been?"

Cletus hung his hat on a peg near the door and straightened as much as his stoop shouldered frame would allow. "What do you mean where have I been? Just because I'm seventy-nine years old don't mean I ain't got things to do. Mmm. Is that coffee I smell?"

Wyatt tried to count to ten. At seven, he shoved his chair back, strode to the filing cabinet and drained the last of the thick brew from the pot. As usual, his show of temper was lost on his grandfather.

Cletus slurped his coffee then slapped Luke on the back. "I haven't had a chance to congratulate you proper yet. I talked to your future bride last night. Said she and Lisa and Mel are goin' into Pierre to look at weddin' dresses this weekend. That's good. Real good. Means plans are movin' along. So, Luke, who're you gonna ask to be your best man?''

Luke glanced up. "Gee, Cletus, I don't rightly know. Clayt or Wyatt, I guess.''

Wyatt's mouth dropped open. Had he just heard Luke say he didn't *rightly* know? For crying out loud, it was enough to turn a grown man's stomach. Gritting his teeth and crossing his arms, he looked at Clayt and said, "He's your brother.''

Clayt shook his head. "He's your best friend.''

With a snap of one suspender, old Cletus said, "Looks like there's only one way to settle this. Okay with you, Luke, if the boys flip for it fair and square?''

Wyatt didn't care who ended up acting as Luke's best man. He was too busy trying to figure out why a woman who claimed she would go out with every man who asked had told *him* that going to dinner wouldn't be a good idea. He wasn't so arrogant as to expect every woman to fall at his feet. He could take no for an answer. But Lisa hadn't told him no. What the hell did she mean going out with him wouldn't be a good idea? Wyatt happened to believe it was the best idea he'd had in years.

Cletus was still talking when Wyatt came out of his musings. "As best man, you'll be expected to hook up with the maid of honor. And Jillian asked Lisa Markman to be her maid of honor, ain't that right, Luke?''

Lisa?

Wyatt jerked to attention. "Heads!'' he called.

"Tails!'' Clayt said at the same time.

Cletus mumbled something about having to do everything himself then flipped the quarter into the air. He caught it easily enough then slapped it against his forearm. Raising his hand slightly, a grin stole across his wrinkled face. "Wyatt, it looks like you're guaranteed at least one weddin' dance with Jillian's dark-haired maid of honor, and maybe a little time alone with her at the barbecue you boys are havin' the first Saturday in September. Oooo-eee, that woman's built for comfort, ain't she?''

Wyatt's mind eased into overdrive. Turning Lisa Markman into his arms for a slow wedding dance was one of the most appealing thoughts he'd had all day. Kissing her for the first time was another, and so was wrapping his arms around her and kissing her again.

"I want to see the coin," Clayt told the older man.

"What do you mean you wanna see the coin?"

"What do you mean what do I mean?"

Wyatt glanced from Cletus to Clayt and back again. His grandfather's brown eyes were spitting daggers at Clayt, but his right hand remained firmly over the coin.

Clayt wasn't budging, either. "It just so happens that I'd trust you with my life, but everyone knows you're not above bending the rules to suit your purposes, and Wyatt *is* your grandson."

"You callin' me a cheater?"

"I'm not calling you anything. Just show us the coin. If Wyatt won fair and square, fine. If not, he can ask Lisa to dance the normal way. She's made it clear she'll give everyone a fair chance. She even went out with Grover Andrews, for cripe's sakes."

Cletus's chin came up a notch, and Wyatt found himself saying a silent prayer that he'd get lucky and a bolt of lightning would strike nearby, or maybe his sainted mother would swoop down from heaven and put her hand over Cletus's mouth.

"That ain't quite true, boy."

Wyatt practically groaned out loud. So much for luck.

"Are you saying Lisa didn't go out with Grover Andrews?" Clayt asked.

"Oh, she went out with Grover, all right. But she ain't gone out with every man who's asked her."

"Who'd she turn down?" Luke asked.

"Yeah, who?" Clayt echoed.

"Didn't Wyatt tell you?"

Clayt and Luke turned like the guards at Buckingham Palace.

"You asked her out?" Luke asked.

"She said no?" Clayt sputtered.

Wyatt heaved a huge sigh. "She didn't say no. Exactly."

"What did she say?" Luke asked.

"She said she didn't think having dinner with me would be a good idea."

"That's odd," Luke said.

"Yeah," Clayt agreed. "Why would a woman who's made it clear that she's looking for the right man say that?"

"Maybe she doesn't think I'm the right man for her."

"How could she possibly know that without going out with you?"

"That's what I've been asking myself all morning."

"I'm tellin' you, boy, you have to stop bein' so nice and take the bull by the horns. Sometimes a man's gotta do what a man's gotta do."

Three pairs of eyes turned to Cletus, three gazes fell to the gnarled hand clutching his arm, and three voices rose at the same time. "That does it."

"Show us that coin."

"Now."

Wyatt had never heard his grandfather utter a more indignant oath, but after looking each younger man straight in the eyes, he finally raised his hand. Wyatt, Clayt and Luke all stared at the shiny quarter resting on Cletus's forearm, but Wyatt was the only one who released a low whistle. "There's no doubt about it, boys. It's heads. I won the toss, fair and square."

Thunder rumbled as Cletus dropped the coin into his

pocket. Turning on the heels of his worn cowboy boots, he strode to the door with all the dignity and speed his skinny, bowed legs could muster.

"Come on, Cletus," Clayt called. "Don't go away mad."

At the door, Cletus mumbled something Wyatt couldn't make out, but he recognized the low, sultry voice that answered. His grandfather stepped to one side and the last woman Wyatt expected to set foot in his office walked through the door.

Anything he might have said froze in his brain. All he could do was stare as Lisa Markman strolled toward him. Looking neither right nor left, she didn't stop until she reached the edge of the railing that divided the office. Wyatt was vaguely aware that Cletus had closed the door behind him, but he didn't take his eyes off the woman wearing the shiny, red raincoat and the churlish expression.

"Sheriff."

"Lisa."

With a haughty lift of her chin, she said, "It's a good thing I don't believe in suing people, or I'd have to file a suit against the town of Jasper Gulch for false advertising."

Wyatt rose to his feet slowly. "Why is that?"

"Your ad said this was a quiet, peaceful town where the biggest crimes are jaywalking and gossip and the ugly color of orange Bonnie Trumble painted the front of her beauty shop."

"And that isn't true?"

She shook her head. "I'm afraid I have to report a theft."

"What's been taken?" Wyatt asked, his voice getting deeper with every word.

Lisa lowered her dripping umbrella then met his wide-eyed stare. "It seems that one of the fine citizens of Jasper Gulch stole my car."

Chapter Two

"Somebody stole your car?" Wyatt asked.

"Thank God."

Wyatt, Luke and Lisa all swung around and looked at Clayt.

"Are you happy about this?" Lisa asked.

Clayt Carson had the grace to look sheepish. "I didn't mean that the way it sounded, ma'am. I'm just relieved because my little girl couldn't have been responsible for stealing a car."

Swiping his faded brown cowboy hat off his head, he glanced at Wyatt and said, "You don't think Haley took it, do you?"

Wyatt settled his hands to his hips and gave Clayt's question careful consideration. The man had every reason to be worried. During the past two months since she'd come to live with her father, nine-year-old Haley Carson had been a handful. She *had* been caught stealing food off Lisa and Jillian's front porch last month, but Wyatt didn't think a little kid was responsible for stealing a car. Even if the child in question *was* Haley Carson. Shifting his gaze to Lisa, he asked, "Did you leave your keys in the ignition?"

She shook her head. "I know most people out here do, but I haven't gotten out of the habit of stashing my keys in my purse every time I get out of my car."

"There you have it," Wyatt told Clayt. "Unless Haley knows how to hot-wire an automobile, she's off the hook."

Clayt crammed his hat back on his head and visibly relaxed. Wyatt slanted his two best friends an arched look. They both looked at Lisa, then at him and then at each other. With half smiles the Carsons were famous for, they tugged at the brims of their hats and muttered something about other places they had to be.

It was all Lisa could do not to shake her head and roll her eyes at the way those two men swaggered out of the office. They couldn't possibly think she'd actually bought their little show of innocence, could they? Oh, she didn't doubt that they had someplace they had to go. After all, there probably were cattle for Luke to inoculate, and Clayt probably did have to get home to his daughter. But those boys were ranchers, not actors, and they left because Wyatt had given them the signal to go.

In the wake of creaking floorboards and the resounding clatter of the door, the room seemed inordinately silent. That silence wrapped around Lisa, as thick as the air before a thunderstorm and just as invigorating.

She wasn't sure why she chose that particular moment to glance up at Wyatt, but once she had, she couldn't look away. This was one of the few times she'd seen him without his white Stetson. His hair was a dark shade of blond. She wasn't surprised it wasn't shaggy around the edges. Oh, no, Wyatt McCully was probably one of those men who got his hair cut the first week of every month just like clockwork. She'd seen his eyes before, so their golden shade of brown came as no surprise, either. Today, she was more concerned about the interest smoldering in their depths.

His skin was as tanned as every other cowboy's she'd met out here. Except Wyatt wasn't a cowboy who wore chaps and spurs. He was the local sheriff. Lisa didn't really care what a man did for a living, and she certainly couldn't fault him for the way he looked in his uniform. It wasn't his beige shirt that put her off. It wasn't even his badge. It was his reputation. According to the grapevine in Jasper Gulch, Wyatt McCully didn't swear, he didn't drink much and didn't chew tobacco. Word had it he'd never gotten in trouble in his entire life.

Lisa Markman had been in plenty. She wasn't ashamed of where she'd been or who she'd become. But she knew what she wanted, what she needed. And she wasn't going to find it in this office.

"Did you know it's bad luck to open an umbrella indoors?"

She glanced from her open umbrella straight into his eyes. "Yes, well, Danger is my middle name."

"Is that a fact?"

Lisa imagined that a lot of female heads had been turned by that deep, rich voice. It was time to let him know he couldn't turn hers. She pressed a button on her umbrella. By the time she'd smoothed the folds into place, she knew how to put an end to the interest in Wyatt's eyes.

"Look, sheriff, if I could have handled this myself, I wouldn't have set foot in this place, but I really need to get my car back. I have a shipment of Western clothes to pick up in Pierre this morning. So, do you think we could get this over with?"

The stiffening of his shoulders was almost imperceptible, and so was the flicker of disappointment way in the back of his eyes. Lisa felt a moment's remorse because she knew she was responsible for both. But she had to hand it to him; there was no resentment or condescension in his attitude.

She would have preferred it if he hadn't called attention to his strength and agility by spinning a high-backed chair around with one hand and effortlessly placing it next to his desk, but she couldn't fault the polite tilt of his head as he motioned for her to take a seat, or the way he moved to the other side of his desk and sat down.

He reached into the bottom drawer and pulled out a form. With pencil in hand, he said, "Let's start with your full name. First, last and middle initial."

She handled the first and last names well enough, but before she could tell him her middle initial, her gaze got stuck on his hands, and her mind floundered. He didn't have the hands of a man who pushed a pencil for a living. His hands were large and callused, his fingers blunt tipped, his knuckles scraped.

"Is your middle initial really *D?*" he asked.

"Yes."

"For *Danger?*"

"It's *D,*" she said automatically, "for Destiny."

Realizing what she'd said, she glanced up and found him watching her. Trying for an even, composed voice, she said, "Really. My name is Lisa Destiny Markman. My parents didn't like me very much."

"Why don't you start at the beginning."

"The beginning?" she asked.

"When were you born?"

"You want me to start at the beginning of my life?"

"I need your date of birth. For the form."

"Oh." She glanced at the sheet of paper in front of him and rattled off the information he'd requested. Being careful not to make any noise releasing the breath she'd been holding, she stared at his down-turned eyes and told herself she was completely unaffected by this man's quiet presence.

Wyatt jotted down information, checking the proper boxes, filling in the usual blanks. His heart beat a steady rhythm that had nothing to do with procedure. If he'd been with anyone else, he might have laughed to ease the tension in the room, but he glanced up from the form and found Lisa watching him. He couldn't have laughed if he'd tried.

Being careful not to snap the pencil lead, he said, "What could your parents have possibly found not to like about you?"

She leaned toward him slightly. Tilting her face at a sassy angle, she said, "I know it's hard to imagine, but I haven't always been this shy and sweet."

"You're right. I do find that hard to believe."

Wyatt heard her quick intake of breath and saw her eyes widen. He'd surprised her. He was amazed at how much satisfaction the knowledge gave him. However, her discomfiture didn't last long. She closed her eyes, squared her shoulders and crossed her legs. Her red raincoat fell open, and Wyatt had his first up-close glimpse of her legs. Her ankles were small, her calves slightly muscular, her knees narrow. The skin just below the hem of her red Western skirt looked soft and supple and oh so touchable. His reaction was eager and as predictable as nightfall. By the time he managed to drag his gaze back to her face, she was staring at him knowingly.

She covered her legs with her coat and cast him an arch look that spoke volumes. "Shall we continue?"

Despite the fact that the room had warmed at least ten degrees and the blood seemed to have left his brain and was heading for a place south of there, Wyatt found himself wondering where Lisa Markman had acquired her spunk, her intelligence and her independent spirit. Before him sat a woman who could smile at whim and think on her feet. She was sassy and appealing, and she knew it.

There weren't many things more stimulating than a woman who recognized her own sensuality.

"If you don't mind, Sheriff, I'd like to get back to the report."

Wyatt reined in his wayward thoughts and did his best to ignore the pulsing knot that had formed low in his stomach. He asked her pertinent questions and finished filling out the form, an indefinable feeling of rightness growing with every breath he took. Lisa might have turned down his invitation to dinner last night, but she was as aware of the attraction between them as he was.

He would have preferred her to be open about her feelings, but he wasn't opposed to a woman playing hard to get. Doing everything in his power to keep the smile of anticipation off his face, he turned the form around and indicated the place for her to sign.

She wrote her name with a flourish, then rose to her feet. Rising, too, he said, "We're not talking about a pie thief here. We're talking about grand theft auto, and I assure you I'll do everything in my power to get to the bottom of it and get your car back to you. Now, how about that dinner I mentioned last night?"

He liked the look of genuine surprise that crossed her face, but when she raised her chin a notch, then paused as if she was searching for the proper words, he had a feeling he was in for another letdown. When she finally spoke, it was in a soft, conciliatory tone of voice he didn't like one bit. "I hope you don't take offense, Sheriff, but I'm afraid you're just not my type."

Wyatt felt his face fall, but she wasn't finished. "Just so you know, I already have plans for the evening. I promised Butch Brunner I'd drive down to Rosebud to watch him ride a bronco at the rodeo tonight."

As if she didn't expect a reply, she turned and strode to the door. Ignoring his earlier warning about bad luck, she opened her umbrella and walked out into the rain.

* * *

Lisa smoothed a wrinkle from the lightweight denim jumper then pressed a tack into the lattice boards that divided the display window from the rest of the store. She knew it was late in the season to try to sell summer clothing, but she was hoping a new display and sale prices would lure the women of Jasper Gulch inside. She wasn't exactly sure how she was going to get to Pierre to pick up the new fall merchandise, now that she was without a car, but she knew she'd find a way just like she always did.

She was probably the only person in the world who would move more than five hundred miles in order to open a clothing store in a town whose population barely reached five hundred during the worst drought in more than two decades. Still, she'd arrived in mid-July full of high hopes and big plans. Other than a flash-in-the-pan sales frenzy in the days before last month's town picnic, business hadn't exactly been booming. But the drought was over, and for now at least, the rain had stopped. Surely that was a good sign.

Melody McCully rapped on the window and waved as she passed by. Since Lisa's hands were full of tacks and a man's Western shirt, she gave Melody a wink and a smile that earned her a gesture that would have been unbecoming on anybody else. Lisa's smile hovered around the edges of her mouth for a long time after she'd turned back to her task.

Mel McCully is nothing like her brother.

She jerked, as much from the thought of Wyatt as from the pain in the tip of the finger that had gotten in the way of one of her strategically placed tacks. Popping her finger into her mouth, she glanced out the window just in time to see Opal Graham and Isabell Pruitt avert their beady eyes and raise their self-righteous little chins.

Lisa recognized the open censure on their faces. For the life of her, she didn't know what she'd done to deserve it.

They hadn't so much as spoken to her, so how could they possibly dislike her? Surely her hopes and dreams weren't so much different than theirs had been when they were her age. At thirty, all Lisa wanted was a home, a family, a way to make ends meet and a man to love. When it came to a home, she wasn't fussy. Any four walls would do. After all, she'd lived in enough places to know that it wasn't the structure that brought security. She knew exactly what she was looking for in a man. Glancing at the racks and shelves containing everything from men's work clothes to women's skirts to children's play clothes, she knew she could make her store a success, too. She just had to be patient.

The bell over the front door jingled. There, see? The customers are starting to come already. She had a smile ready before she could turn around.

Louetta Graham mumbled a shy greeting then quickly averted her eyes. Glancing at her watch, Lisa toned down the brightness of her smile a little and said, "Goodness, Louetta, I had no idea it was eleven-thirty already. Your arrival is just like clockwork."

"I'm sorry. I didn't mean to bother you."

Lisa did everything in her power to soften her smile even more. Honestly, she'd never come across anyone more shy than Opal Graham's daughter. Every time she saw Louetta, Lisa thought of a stray cat. Maybe it was her drab brown hair; or maybe it was the way she skirted the edges of a room to keep from coming face-to-face with anyone.

"Well. Um. I guess I'll be going," she whispered, her eyes on the old brown floorboards at her feet.

"You don't have to go," Lisa murmured. "You're more than welcome to browse. Business has been kind of slow lately, and I look forward to your visits to my store."

"You do?"

Lisa nodded.

"I'm glad, because coming here is the highlight of my day."

Louetta flushed, and Lisa hid a smile to herself. Those were the most words she'd heard Louetta string together since she'd started coming here at exactly eleven-thirty a.m. five days ago.

According to Melody, Louetta was thirty-three years old. She looked older and acted younger. She was a little taller than Lisa, which would probably make her about the same height as Jillian, who was five-seven. Although it was difficult to tell underneath those long, baggy skirts and loose-fitting, high-collared blouses, Louetta probably had an ample bosom and long legs. The woman was as plain as plain could be, but she really was sweet.

"Is there anything I could help you find?" Lisa asked.

"Oh, no," Louetta said hurriedly. "I'm just looking."

"You just go right ahead and look to your heart's content."

Fifteen minutes later, Lisa had finished straightening the display of men's jeans and Louetta was working her way toward the front of the store. Reaching for a hanger, Lisa said, "One day soon I'll be getting in my new merchandise. I'd planned to pick it up today, but it looks like I'm going to have to make other arrangements."

"Yes," Louetta said, nodding for all she was worth. "I heard about your car. I feel really bad, too. Now Mother and Isabell are going to be able to tell everyone 'I told you so.'"

Louetta's hazel eyes grew round seconds before a blush climbed up her face. Covering her cheeks with her hands, she said, "I shouldn't have said that."

Thrusting her hands to her hips, Lisa said, "Now Louetta, you haven't told me anything I didn't already know. I was sitting right there when old Isabell stood up at the town meeting last night." Doing her best impression of a person with nasal problems, Lisa raised one finger and spouted, "'Ill will come of that advertisement luring women to our peaceful town. Harlots and women of ill repute, that's what that ad will draw. Mark my words.'"

Louetta's eyes grew large. "Doesn't that hurt your feelings?"

Dropping her hands to her sides, Lisa shrugged. "You know what they say about sticks and stones breaking bones."

Lisa followed Louetta's gaze to the toes of her sensible shoes. "I think that that saying is all wrong. I think names really can hurt. Well," she added in a voice that was so quiet Lisa had to strain to hear, "I have to get back to the library."

The bell over the door jingled when Louetta left, but Lisa stayed where she was, lost in thought. People had a way of amazing her. They always had. She remembered one educational summer she'd spent waitressing in an elite restaurant in Chicago. She'd made more in tips in one night than she made in an entire week anywhere else. The men who dined there wore suits a person simply didn't find at the mall, and the women wore gowns, not dresses. They had everything: education, sophistication and money. At first sight they were the most beautiful people Lisa had ever seen. But by dessert their true colors usually reared, and it wasn't a pretty picture. The contrast between those men and women and Louetta Graham was truly amazing. What was even more amazing was the fact that someone who was as plain as day could say something so profound that her true beauty began to emerge.

I think names really can hurt.

Louetta was right. Names were words, and words wielded incredible power. They could nurture, they could heal, and they could destroy. They were so important they even had a constitutional amendment to protect them. It was too bad folks didn't have the same kind of protection from the people who used words in a harmful, hurtful way.

Glancing at her quiet store with all its racks of blue jeans and Western shirts, Lisa wondered if she'd hurt Wyatt's feelings when she'd so blatantly told him he wasn't her type. She hadn't said it to hurt him. She'd only wanted to set him straight where she was concerned. Unfortunately, the fact that she'd had good intentions didn't make it right. Wyatt McCully hadn't said or done anything to warrant her curt attitude. He hadn't really even said or done anything to lead her to believe he was interested in her in more than a friendly way. It wasn't his fault her hormones went on red alert every time she looked at him. So he'd asked her to dinner. There was no law against that. Thirteen other bachelors had done the same thing, and she hadn't gotten all bristly with them.

Wyatt was an honorable, steadfast man, which was exactly why he wasn't her type. Still, if she had it to do over again, she would handle the situation in a way that wouldn't hurt such a nice, kind, patient man's feelings.

A horn blared out on the street. Lisa peeked around her new display just in time to see a patrol car pull up to the curb. Behind the wheel that nice, kind, patient man she had just been thinking about was laying on the horn.

She was out of the store in an instant. Leaning down in order to peer through the open window on the passenger side of the car, she said, "Wyatt, what in the world are you doing?"

"Get in."

"What?" she asked.

"Get in."

"Now why would I want to do that?"

His eyes darkened as he held her gaze. "Because I have business in Pierre and I figured you might as well ride along to pick up your merchandise."

"I see."

"I highly doubt that. I'll give you a ride to Pierre. And like I said before, I have every intention of getting your car back for you. Since I doubt that'll happen by tonight, you'll have to find another ride down to the rodeo in Rosebud, because that's where I draw the line.''

Lisa hadn't expected Wyatt to be the type who drew invisible lines. She hadn't expected him to be the type who didn't let a person get a word in edgewise, either. But evidently he was on a roll.

"I'm supposed to be in Pierre in thirty minutes. And it's a forty-minute drive. Are you coming?"

He didn't say, "Or aren't you?" but he might as well have. She stared at him for a full five seconds, amazed to find that the good sheriff had an ornery side.

Much to her surprise, she grinned. With a mock salute and her famous wink, she called, "Aye-aye, sir."

Still smiling, she dashed away to get her purse and lock the store.

Lisa glanced over her shoulder at the boxes stacked in the back of the cruiser, then settled herself more comfortably in her seat. The check she'd written to pay for the new merchandise had nearly scraped the bottom of her bank account. But her rent was paid through the end of the year, and if she watched her spending, she might be able to make it until the store started showing a profit.

Keeping her fingers wrapped firmly around the hair at her nape, she turned her face into the warm air streaming through the open window and watched the scenery going by. This was definitely ranching country. The land was mostly flat, with occasional rolling hills dotted with small herds of cattle. The ranch houses were few and far between, rough-hewn fences and telephone poles stretching as far as the eye could see.

From the corner of her eye she saw Wyatt shift in his seat and rotate a kink out of his shoulders. She'd done everything in her power to cajole him out of his dark mood. So far she hadn't been successful. That was unusual. People almost always responded to her sultry laughs and brash smiles. Evidently, the good sheriff was holding a grudge.

Trying to fill the silence stretching between them, she pointed to a gray wall of clouds on the horizon. "It looks like another thunderstorm is forming."

He made a sound that meant yes, then fell silent once again. Lisa wanted to scream. She'd heard of yup and nope talkers, but this was ridiculous. Trying again, she said, "That's good, isn't it? Those clouds have a lot of dry weather to make up for. Maybe the ranchers out here won't starve this winter after all. Maybe I won't, either."

She felt his eyes on her, but by the time she turned her head, he was watching the road again, his fingers looped around the steering wheel. Releasing a pent-up breath of air, she said, "No, business hasn't really been very good. It's so kind of you to ask."

Wyatt bit down on the inside of one cheek, doing everything in his power to hold on to his vexation. Not that Lisa was making it easy. She'd been sultry and warm and more than a little brash since the moment they'd pulled away from the curb in front of her store an hour and a half ago. Whether she believed him or not, he had a lot on his mind.

Earlier he'd driven to her place on Elm Street to take a look around. The rain had washed away any tire tracks there might have been in the gravel driveway, but there was one faint impression left in the mud by a cowboy boot. Wyatt had measured it against his own foot. Although the print was smaller than his size twelve boots, it wasn't much help. Other than Clayt and Luke, practically every man in the county had a smaller boot size than his. Lisa's neighbors hadn't seen or heard anything out of the ordinary. Whoever had taken that car hadn't left many clues. Wyatt had been giving the matter a great deal of thought.

People out here just didn't steal cars. Or at least they never had. Why would someone steal Lisa's?

He'd been giving the curt little declaration she'd made concerning his invitation to dinner a lot of thought, too. She had a smile that could warm him twenty degrees and a laugh that took his fantasies to another level entirely. And her body, well. She filled out her shirt to perfection, and he'd bet his badge that every last inch of her was the real thing. He'd lain awake imagining how her breasts would feel beneath his hands, his mouth. Wyatt McCully wasn't exactly a ladies' man, but no matter what she said, no matter what she claimed, the attraction between them was mutual.

"You know, Wyatt," she grumbled, "although I truly appreciate the ride into Pierre and the little lunch you treated me to, this trip would go a lot faster if you'd keep up your end of the conversation."

He glanced at her, and found her looking out the window. One hand was on her seat belt, the other was holding her hair in a low ponytail at her nape. The breeze streaming through the window toyed with the strands surrounding her face. He liked the way the wind pressed her plain white T-shirt against her body, but he had to admit he liked her straightforwardness just as much.

"Okay."

She turned her head slowly. "What do you mean 'okay'?" she asked, suspicion raising her voice and widening her eyes.

He managed to keep a smile off his face, because she had every reason to be suspicious. "Okay," he repeated. "I'll see what I can do about keeping up my end of the conversation."

"You will?"

He nodded. He didn't see any harm in talking. In fact, talking might just lead to a little insight and a lot of understanding.

Turning off the highway near Capa, he said, "Do you have any theories as to why business hasn't been very good so far?"

"The economy hasn't exactly been the greatest since I moved to town, you know? I think the drought has made everyone leery of spending a dollar they might need to feed their families next winter."

Wyatt hadn't realized he'd gripped the steering wheel tighter, but Lisa must have noticed because she was watching him closely. This time his silence hadn't been intentional. He was always quiet when he crossed the bridge spanning the Bad River. Today, the river wasn't the only thing on his mind.

Wyatt was a rancher's son and a rancher's grandson. He'd grown up in a family that had relied on elements like rain and snow and bottomed-out beef prices to make a living. He'd gone without new shoes and new clothes on more than one occasion. To this day, he remembered how his father used to say, "You can wear secondhand clothes, but you can't eat secondhand food."

Most of the folks out here had their priorities firmly in order. Even though Lisa hadn't been here long, she'd put her finger on the pulse that made these people who they were. He didn't know why, but the fact that she seemed to understand them on an instinctive, fundamental level made his heart feel two sizes larger.

Pointing to a place a hundred yards downstream, he said, "My parents drowned on the other side of that bend in the river."

Wyatt clamped his mouth shut. For crying out loud, where had that come from? He sure hadn't intended to tell her that. He wanted a response from her, but he wasn't looking for sympathy, not by a long shot.

"Do you want to tell me how it happened?" she asked.

He tried to square his shoulders against her allure, but he made the mistake of looking into her eyes, and he was lost. Aw, hell. Now that he'd brought it up, there wasn't much else he could do except finish it. Staring straight ahead, he said, "They were crossing an old bridge after a spring downpour. The river was dangerously high, but my mother was sick, and my father was trying to get her to the clinic in Pierre. The river took out the bridge, and them with it."

Wyatt had been eleven that year. Since then, he'd experienced a lot of important days in his life. The day he graduated from high school, the day he first pinned on his badge, the day he stood up as Clayt's best man. But he'd never experienced another day that was as vivid and clear in his mind as that day had been.

"What were they like?"

"They were honest, hardworking folks. My father's name was Joe, my mother's was Eleanor. Everyone called her Ellie. They were good people, and like most ranchers around here, they were used to doing without. I guess some things never change. The bachelors can attest to that. We've certainly had to get used to doing without, and I can't think of anybody who's happy about it, except maybe Isabell."

Lisa laughed. It was the last thing he'd expected her to do, but it made him feel a little taller, a little broader. Her laugh was deep, throaty, sexy. It let him know that she was well aware of exactly what it was he'd been doing without.

"I'm sorry, Wyatt. I don't mean to seem irreverent about what happened to your parents. Tragedy has a way of shaping us, forever changing us. It's just that I think you're right. Old Isabell is probably as pleased as punch about your, er, predicament."

Heat crept through him. He knew where it came from, and he knew where it was headed. He hadn't been exaggerating. The nights out here had grown longer and lonelier with every passing month. In its heyday some thirty years ago, Jasper Gulch had had more than seven hundred residents. With the steady departure of its single women these past three decades, the number barely reached five hundred today. Sixty-two of the current residents were bachelors between the ages of twenty and seventy-five. Until Lisa and Jillian's arrival last month, and a handful of single women since, there had only been six marriageable women.

Feeling her eyes on him, he said, "Then you believe me when I say we've suffered?"

She turned her head, but not before he saw her smile. "Oh, I believe you. I'm just a little surprised so many women left, that's all."

"In case you haven't noticed, there aren't many job prospects out here, other than becoming a rancher's wife, that is. The girls who left didn't want the seclusion of a rancher's life. They wanted more."

"I'm surprised at least one of them didn't want you."

Lisa clamped her lips together, thinking her mouth was going to be the death of her yet. It had gotten her into a lot of trouble over the years. Until about five seconds ago, she'd thought she'd outgrown it. Since there wasn't much she could do except look at Wyatt to gauge his reaction, she turned her head.

She was in trouble all right. His eyes had closed partway and had warmed to a darker shade of brown. One corner of his mouth lifted, creasing one lean cheek. If she'd been a woman who played games, she would have touched that crease with the back of her finger. But she hadn't come all the way to Jasper Gulch to play games. She came to start over and to find a man like her.

No matter how interested Wyatt was, no matter how that interest made her feel, she knew what she had to do. This time she'd do it in a way that didn't hurt his feelings.

She was still trying to find the proper words when he

said, "Now that you know about my past, how about telling me about yours?"

Lisa's mind cleared, and her objectivity returned. She'd been searching frantically for a way to put an end to his interest once and for all. Unknowingly he'd handed her the perfect opportunity. Now if she could just bring herself to talk about her least favorite subject in all the world.

Pretending to watch the scenery going by, she said, "What would you like to know?"

Chapter Three

"For starters," Wyatt said in a voice just loud enough to be heard over the country-western song playing on the radio, "you could tell me where you grew up."

Lisa tried to concentrate on the way the wind whipped her hair into her eyes. She tried to imagine how long it was going to take to get the tangles out, and how much work she had ahead of her emptying boxes once she got back to the store. She tried to think about anything that didn't have to do with her childhood. But Wyatt had asked, and she knew she'd answer, eventually.

She would have preferred him to ask why she'd decided to come to South Dakota or why she'd wanted to open a clothing store or how she'd earned her living before moving out here. But people always seemed more interested in where she'd been and what she'd done a long time ago.

Taking a deep breath, she began in the usual way. "I was born in Chicago, but I grew up in a lot of places."

"Did your parents move around when you were a kid?"

"I moved around on my own." If she'd looked at him,

she probably would have seen questions in his eyes, but she had to hand it to him, he didn't pry.

Since she had good reason for telling him about her childhood, she waded through a few more moments of silence then said, "I ran away a couple of days before I turned fifteen."

He didn't ask why. He didn't ask how. He simply waited for her to continue. After a while she said, "Come on, Sheriff, you must be dying to know *why* I ran away."

He seemed to be taking his time searching for the appropriate reply. By the time he spoke, they'd reached the village limits on the north end of town. "I'd be surprised if you didn't have good reasons for doing what you did. Did you ever go back?"

It wasn't the question people normally asked at this point. It confused her and sent a strange, disquieting feeling through her. He didn't know her very well, yet he seemed to believe in her. What was a woman supposed to do with a man like that?

Staring at the hard, lean lines of his profile, she said, "I went back a few times. The cops' idea, not mine. But I always left again."

Wyatt could see Lisa out of the corner of his eye. She'd let go of her hair, and it was whipping across her face, into her eyes and mouth. He'd wondered where she'd acquired her strength and her independence of spirit. He was beginning to get a pretty good idea. In his mind he pictured a police officer dragging a skinny girl whose dark brown eyes were too big for her face back to a place she didn't want to go. Something told him she wouldn't have been a willing passenger. Oh, no, Lisa Markman had probably gone back kicking and screaming bloody murder.

"No wonder you're leery of a man wearing a badge."

"What makes you think that?"

It was his turn to be surprised. "You implied that."

"No, I didn't."

"Then you don't dislike men in uniform?" he asked.

"Of course not."

"What about me? Do you dislike me?"

"I think you're very nice."

Easing into a small, tentative smile, he said, "Nice enough to take in dinner and a movie with me?"

"Too nice for that."

Suddenly the word *nice* sounded as grating as fingernails scraping a blackboard. "I beg your pardon?" he croaked.

Her hands covered her cheeks. "Oh, my gosh. I've done it again, haven't I? I'm sorry if that sounded like an insult. It was far from intentional. You really are a very nice man. You're like one of those good guys on TV, right down to your white hat. You probably go to bed by eleven every night and to church every Sunday. Heck, you were probably a choirboy when you were a kid. Now that you know about my past, you should understand why I'm looking for someone completely different."

It took a lot to make Wyatt mad, but no matter what she said, he was no saint. He clamped his mouth shut and jerked the car to a stop in a parking space in front of the store. He threw the gearshift into Park, got out, kicked his door shut and gave the back door a yank. Slightly dismayed, Lisa got out, too. Hoisting a heavy box into his arms, Wyatt looked at her over the top of his car. The smile she attempted did nothing to put him in a better frame of mind.

"Look," she said, carrying a smaller box to the front door, "I probably didn't say any of that the way I should have. I didn't mean to hurt your feelings."

Instead of replying, he waited for her to unlock the door, then plowed past her into the store and dropped the box on the floor, only to stride back out to the sidewalk to get another. Lisa figured there was nothing like anger to light a fire underneath a man's feet. By the time the trunk and back seat were empty, Wyatt had made two trips for every one of hers. And he still hadn't uttered a word.

She felt horrid, but for the life of her she didn't know what to do or say to make things right. Still, she had to try. "Look, Sheriff—"

He stopped abruptly. Spinning around, he hiked the box to one hip and scooped his hat off his head. "If you're thinking about apologizing again, there's no need. Your opinion of me is certainly humbling, but no matter what you think, I don't spend all my time rescuing kittens out of trees."

"Of course you don't. I didn't mean to imply—"

"For your information, I broke up a band of cattle thieves a few years back, and I once arrested a bank robber down in Westover."

Wyatt crammed his hat on his head and hid a world-size cringe. Why didn't he bring up the trophy he took for roping calves when he was thirteen, for cripe's sakes?

They stared at each other. Neither of them smiled or moved or said a word. Her dark hair was messed, wispy tendrils framing her face in total disarray. Wyatt imagined it would look much the same after a long night of making love. He spent so much time on that thought he had to remind himself to breathe, but he certainly didn't have to remind himself what the heat coursing through him meant.

Watching the play of emotions cross her face, he couldn't help wondering what she was thinking. If their hearts weren't beating the same rhythm he would eat his hat. She may have thought he was nice on an intellectual level, but physically her body was thrumming with something much more earthy and sensual and wild, and so was his. He moved closer, his breathing a husky rasp in his own ears, his eyes trained on her mouth, his thoughts slowing to only one.

A sound near the door stopped his forward motion. Wyatt glanced up as Cletus rushed in, winded. "Boy, I've been waiting for you to get back for hours."

"What is it, Granddad?"

"Mertyl Gentry's fit to be tied. She was almost in tears the last time she called. Made me promise I'd tell you the second you pulled into town."

Wyatt nodded abruptly, hoping the gesture would spur his grandfather to tell him what the old woman was upset about. Mertyl Gentry was a seventy-eight-year-old widow who'd lived in the same house on Pike Street for sixty years. A few days ago he would have assumed she was calling to complain about neighbor kids trampling her flowers. Now that he knew a car thief was on the loose, he wasn't so quick to dismiss the possibility of something much more serious.

"Is Mertyl all right?" he asked.

"Far as I know."

Wyatt glanced at Lisa and found her eyes mirroring his own concern. "Granddad," he sputtered. "Are you going to tell me or aren't you?"

Cletus snapped his suspenders and raised his craggy chin. "I'm gettin' to it, I'm gettin' to it. Ya don't hafta get huffy. It's that confounded cat of hers. Went and got himself stuck up in a tree again. Mertyl says you're the only person she trusts to get him down safe and sound."

Adrenaline seeped out of Wyatt like a tire with a leaky valve. He vacillated between dropping his head into his hands and telling Mertyl Gentry to get her own stupid cat out of her tree.

"What's the matter, boy? Cat got your tongue?"

Wyatt wished his grandfather had used some other cliché. He glanced at Lisa and found her looking back at him. She didn't say a word, but the lift of her eyebrows spoke volumes.

Clenching his teeth, he hoisted the last box onto a table.

He gave Lisa and Cletus a curt nod, then stomped out the door.

His grandfather's gravelly voice reached his ears. "Now what do you s'pose has gotten into him?"

The door slammed on Lisa's reply. For all Wyatt cared, she could tell Cletus the truth, that she thought his only grandson was a lily-livered choirboy. For her information he only sang in the shower, and even then he couldn't carry a tune in a basket.

He slammed the trunk closed, then climbed into the sheriff car and started the engine. Lord, he was ticked. Actually he was mad as hell. If Cletus had given him five more seconds, Wyatt would have made his move. The memory of the anticipation that had strummed through him at the look in Lisa's eyes was potent and clear. Just five more seconds and he would have reached for her hand and drawn her closer, five more seconds and he would have wrapped his arms around her and lowered his mouth to hers.

Just five measly seconds.

Cletus McCully had a lot of good qualities, but the man had lousy timing.

Driving south on Main Street, Wyatt waved to the old-timers who had gathered in front of Ed's Barber Shop, but the gesture was halfhearted. He made a left on Pike Street, pulling to a stop in front of Mertyl Gentry's small white house. The frail, gray-haired lady met him on the porch and ushered him into the backyard as if he hadn't done this a dozen times before. The thought brought his anger crashing through him all over again.

Stifling an oath, he shimmied up Mertyl's oak tree. Other than the small branch that caught on his hat, sending it sailing to the ground, the climb was uneventful. He crawled out on a high limb and rescued the cat, only to get scratched and spit at for his trouble. It took every ounce of restraint he possessed to keep from spitting right back.

Watching him closely, Mertyl took her orange tabby from him the second he reached the ground. In a singsongy voice, she cooed, "There, there, Daisy, you're safe now. Poor baby." The way she tucked the overweight cat into the folds of her flowered cotton house robe made it perfectly clear that she felt Wyatt posed as much of a threat as the blasted tree.

He scooped his hat off the ground, exchanged a few words with Mertyl, then drove back to the office, the word *nice* playing through his mind like a broken record. *Nice.* Lisa thought he was nice. Puppies were nice. Spring flowers were nice. Comfortable old clothes were nice. So were little old ladies and homemade chicken soup.

Suddenly, *nice* sounded boring and annoying as hell.

He climbed out of his car and strode into the office, slamming the door behind him in a not-so-*nice* way. He checked his messages, then tossed his hat onto a hook on the wall.

Lisa thought he was nice? Fine. She could think any stinking thing she wanted. He was through working his tail off to impress her. He had some pride, after all. Somewhere. Besides, there were other fish in the sea. Okay. There weren't many. And there were none who could speed up his heart rate with a simple lift of her eyebrows. But it didn't matter. Wyatt McCully had made up his mind. He was a man, and had a man's sensitive ego. He wasn't going to get dropped on his rear over that woman again.

And that was final.

"Clayt. Give me your chaps," Wyatt said a few hours later.

"Give you my what?" Clayt groused.

Wyatt slanted his friend a narrow look then regarded his surroundings in silence. An announcer's voice echoed over the loudspeakers. Spectators were cheering on a barrel racer in another arena. A few feet away horses whinnied and nickered. A little farther off the beaten track, Clayt's daughter, Haley, was jumping mud puddles with a couple of boys her age.

Turning his attention back to the situation at hand, Wyatt said, "I'm going to ride High Kicker, and I need your chaps."

"Are you crazy? I rode him a little while ago. That bronc bucked me off faster than a buckle bunny can shed her clothes. Since when have you decided to participate in the rodeo?"

Wyatt's eyes shifted to the dark-haired woman taking her seat halfway up the stands on the other side of the arena. He'd been toying for an hour with the idea of riding the bronc, but he'd made up his mind two minutes ago when Lisa had planted a kiss on Butch Brunner's mouth after he'd gotten himself thrown three or four seconds into his ride.

Following the course of Wyatt's stare, Clayt said, "Tell me you aren't really going to climb on a bronco and make a complete fool of yourself over a woman."

Wyatt didn't bother to try to hide his dark expression. Staring at Lisa, he said, "Sometimes a man's gotta do what a man's gotta do."

Clayt Carson regarded Wyatt for a long time. Since Wyatt had been on the receiving end of his friend's shrewd looks too often to let it rattle him, he let Clayt look to his heart's content.

"I'll be doggoned," Clayt declared, shaking his head.

"You can be anything you want. Now, what do you say about those chaps?"

Clayt's grin may have been slow in coming, but it was as steady as his hands as he began to undo the buckles and laces on his chaps. "I say 'cowboy up,' partner."

"Now do you see why the rodeo is the number one spectator sport in South Dakota?" Melody McCully asked.

It took a lot to overwhelm Lisa, but the sounds and scents and activity going on all around her came close to doing just that. The smell of roasting hot dogs, greasy French fries and doughy elephant ears permeated the air. She was pretty sure people could hear the announcers all the way to Wyoming, and she'd never seen so many cowboy hats in one place in her life. She'd never seen so many cowboys hit the ground so hard you could practically hear their bones crunch, either.

Casting Mel a questioning look, Lisa said, "This is my first rodeo, but it's interesting, that's for sure. See that cowboy down there? Five minutes ago he used language that practically curled my hair, but a second or two before his horse bucked him off I swear I heard him chant a prayer to the Virgin Mother. Tell me again why perfectly sensible men climb onto the backs of raging bulls and wild horses whose life ambition is to throw them off again as fast and painfully as possible."

"Please. Don't say that word."

"What word?"

Mel mouthed the word *virgin*.

"What's wrong with the word *virgin?*" Lisa asked.

Mel shuddered. "Nothing. It's just that I'm going to turn thirty in a couple of months and—never mind."

For the first time since Lisa had arrived at the rodeo an hour ago, the noise and confusion all around her receded, and all her attention was trained on the blond woman sitting next to her. Melody McCully had been the second person to welcome Lisa and Jillian into town last month, and in the days since, she'd become a wonderful friend. She wore blue jeans most of the time and ran her diner the way a captain ran a tight ship. She could cuss like a sailor, too, which was amazing, considering she was Wyatt's younger sister.

There wasn't much to Mel, but what there was was strong. Her eyes were light blue, her mouth equally prone to smiling and sputtering. Lisa couldn't help wondering how many people had taken the time to look underneath all that dander where a gentler spirit was hiding.

"Mel, are you telling me you're a virgin?" Lisa asked quietly.

"I asked you not to say that word." Mel's voice trailed away and returned seconds later. "So what if I am?"

Lisa grinned at Mel's stern-faced expression. "There's nothing wrong with it."

"Are you laughing at me?"

"Of course not. I'm just a little surprised, that's all. It *is* supposed to be unusual in this day and age, you know, especially for a woman like you."

"If that was intended as a compliment, it needs a little work."

Lisa laughed again, thinking that Mel McCully was more like her brother than she'd realized. Just like that, Lisa's laughter stopped. She squared her shoulders and closed her eyes and wished to high heaven she could stop thinking about Melody's brother.

Flashing Mel a conciliatory grin, she said, "Sorry. I seem to be making a habit of sticking my foot in my mouth today. Believe it or not, that was supposed to be a compliment. I've been a lot of places, and I haven't come across many women as strong and pretty and as sure of themselves as you are who are still virgins, that's all."

"You think I'm pretty?"

Leave it to Mel to pick that out of everything else Lisa had said. Nodding, she asked, "Don't you?"

Mel fingered the hair in her braid, her gaze on something in the distance. Following the course of her stare, Lisa saw Clayt Carson leaning on a gate, one foot hiked on a low rung, his arms crossed along the top board.

Lowering her voice to a whisper, Lisa said, "The bachelors out here must be blind."

"Not blind," Melody answered. "Just hardheaded and stubborn as mules. What about you?"

Lisa turned her head so fast she saw stars. "Are you asking me if I'm hardheaded or stubborn as a mule?"

Mel shook her head. "I was wondering if you were— Never mind. It's none of my business."

"What?" Lisa insisted.

"Well," Mel said, shrugging one shoulder. "I was just wondering if you were a, you know, a *v-i-r-g-i-n.*"

Several trite sayings raced through Lisa's mind. She couldn't seem to get any of them past the lump that had formed in her throat. Most people took one look at the way she filled out her shirt and automatically assumed she was easy. When they heard her life story they were sure that she'd had plenty of experience. The fact that Mel hadn't prejudged her sent a strange feeling to Lisa's chest.

Melody jumped to her feet and let loose a holler that had half the spectators turning in their seats to look at them. For a moment Lisa thought it was because of their little conversation, but how could it have been? She hadn't answered Melody's question.

"Lisa, look over there."

With her mind still a little foggy, Lisa stood, too. Normally it took a while to distinguish one cowboy hat from another. Most of the men she'd met wore hats that were brown or black or gray. She only knew one man who wore a white Stetson.

"Mel, that looks like Wyatt."

"That *is* Wyatt," Mel sputtered. "What in tarnation do you suppose my brother is doing climbing into the chute with a bucking bronco?"

The announcer's voice boomed over the loudspeakers, drowning out anything Lisa might have said. "Hold on to your seats, ladies and gentlemen. It looks like one of the notorious Jasper Gents is going to try his luck on High Kicker."

* * *

Wyatt's hat shaded his eyes from the setting sun, but it did nothing to relieve the tension that had his heart beating a mile a minute and his nerves standing on end. Normally he sat through the segment of the program when the announcer asked for audience participation from any non-professional rodeo rider wishing to test his stamina on the back of a bucking bronco. But this wasn't a normal evening. Tonight his reputation was on the line, at least where one confounded, stubborn brunette was concerned. Sweat trickled down the side of his face. Trying to remember everything he'd ever learned about riding one of these ornery creatures, he gripped the single rein in his left hand and raised his right hand into the air.

The chute clanked open, and the bronc lurched through. Somehow Wyatt managed to go with it.

He'd spent countless hours on a horse over the years. He'd gone on roundups where he'd sat in a saddle until his back and legs were so stiff he could hardly move. First his father, and then his grandfather, had taught him how to break in horses that had no intention of being ridden. Like practically every other man out here, he'd done a little rodeoing in his day, and he always tried his luck on the mechanical bull DoraLee brought into the Crazy Horse every summer. But that mechanical bull was nothing like the live wire underneath him right now.

High Kicker had earned his name. He sprang straight into the air, all four hooves coming off the ground, his body twisting and writhing, his ears laid back, his teeth bared. Wyatt's father used to brag that his son had a natural ability to find a horse's center and ride just above it. The muscles in Wyatt's legs strained to hold tight while he tried to make his father proud one more time.

It took incredible concentration to keep his right hand high, his knees bent and his butt in the saddle. The wild horse was doing everything in his power to buck Wyatt off. The bronc jerked to the right, to the left, bringing his head down, his hind legs up then back down again with so much force it rattled Wyatt's bones. Blood rushed through his head, drowning out the cry of the crowd and the booming voice over the loudspeaker.

He imagined Lisa's kiss and held on tighter.

The object of saddle bronc riding was to stay on the horse for at least eight seconds. Surely he'd been out here ten times that long. The muscles in his legs shook; the fingers in his glove cramped. High Kicker jerked his head down and kicked up his hind legs then practically buckled in two. A bell sounded. The horse reared, and Wyatt was airborne.

He must have remembered to let go of the rein, because when he somersaulted through the air, his hand was empty. Some bronc riders claimed they felt like they were falling in slow motion. Wyatt hit the ground so fast he didn't know what end was up. He did, however, know which end of him was hurting, and it wasn't the end that contained his pride.

"Wyatt McCully, ladies and gentlemen," the announcer yelled. "It looks as if the sheriff of Jones County could make his living as a professional rodeo rider if he ever wanted to give up the high life and hit the road."

Wyatt found his feet and looked around. Like most boys growing up in South Dakota, he'd once harbored the dream of becoming one of those bandy-legged rodeo champions who had equal amounts of gumption and broken bones. But no more. He'd never had much wanderlust running through his veins, and he sure as hell hadn't climbed into that chute because he was looking to make a career change. He'd done it for a much more invigorating reason. After brushing off the seat of his pants and scooping his hat out of the mud, he raised his hand to the crowd then strode to the gate where his reason was waiting.

* * *

"Are you trying to get yourself killed?" Mel shouted from the other side of the gate.

He shook his head at his sister, but barely took his eyes off the woman standing next to her. Lisa's jeans were the color of buckskin, her tank top a shade or two lighter. He'd never seen anybody who could make brown look so good.

"Well?" Lisa asked. "Are you?"

He took his time letting his gaze climb to her face. What he saw when he got there made him forget all about the ache in his lower back. Her eyes held a sheen of purpose that made his heart pound. Flicking the mud from his hat, he cocked his head to one side and said, "I didn't know you cared."

She snorted in a most unbecoming way. "I care about all God's creatures, no matter how stupid."

Wyatt grinned all over again. "Did you tell Butch Brunner he was stupid before you kissed *him?*"

Something about the way he accented his question made everything inside Lisa go momentarily still. A devilish look came into his eyes, playing havoc with her senses. "What makes you think I'd kiss you?"

He glanced behind him. Finding the arena empty, he leaned on the gate and said, "Oh, I don't know. But it does seem like the fair thing for you to do, don't you agree?"

Try as she might, she couldn't quite bring herself to bristle. She could, however, lower her chin and her voice and say, "I thought I made my position perfectly clear."

"Ah, yes. You think I'm nice."

He climbed up the gate and vaulted over. Holding her spellbound with his gaze, he planted his boots firmly on the ground, removed his leather glove with his teeth, then slowly reached for her hand.

She knew she should do something, try to speak or move, anything to keep Wyatt from coming any closer, to keep his lips from parting and his eyes from taking on the

dreamy haze of a man with kissing on his mind. But she
didn't do any of those things. She couldn't. Dazed, she
raised her chin, tilted her head a little and let her eyelashes
drift partway down.

Up close she could see the tiny lines beside his eyes,
and the late-day stubble on his chin. He smelled of man
and mud and horse, and something else that was infinitely
elusive and much more appealing. She closed her eyes,
and his lips touched hers, gently at first and then with more
pressure, more feeling, more fire.

She'd kissed a dozen men these past few months, but
none of them had prepared her for Wyatt. She'd tried to
tell herself a sheriff whose reputation was squeaky clean
would only give chaste kisses. There was nothing chaste
about the lips on hers. Passion inched through her veins,
fluttering at every pulse point, churning a hunger inside
her that was in stark contrast to her vow to remain unaffected.

She hadn't realized she'd slid her hands around his neck
until she felt his hair beneath her fingertips. As if it was
all the invitation he needed, Wyatt glided his arms around
her back, pulling her hard against him. She wasn't really
shocked at the rasp of his labored breathing or his eager
response to the brush of her body against his; she was
shocked at hers.

Good heavens, what was she doing?

Turning her head, she broke the kiss, letting her hands
fall away from his neck. Suddenly aware of the voices over
the loudspeakers and the roar of the crowd as yet another
local cowboy tried his hand at riding a bronc, she stepped
back and glanced at Mel. Her friend was doing a pretty
good job of pretending that she hadn't watched the whole
thing. Lisa would deal with Mel later. Right now she had
to deal with Wyatt.

She looked up at him and was filled with a curious longing all over again. The rodeo went on around them, but Lisa couldn't seem to concentrate on anything except the light in his eyes. "That shouldn't have happened, Wyatt."

"Did you tell Butch Brunner that when you kissed him?" he asked with far too much self-confidence for Lisa's peace of mind.

She wished he'd stop comparing his kiss to Butch's. Of course she didn't tell Butch Brunner that. That kiss had lasted a matter of seconds, and hadn't sent a primitive yearning all the way to her toes.

The man standing before her had the loose-jointed look of an honest-to-goodness cowboy. His hips were thrust forward, his stance wide beneath the leather chaps. His shirt was sweat stained, his hat was dirty, and his eyes were crinkled at the corners as if he'd spent years peering out over the horizon.

But Wyatt McCully wasn't a cowboy, and it would be wise to remember that. Forcing herself to think rationally, she said, "Why did you ride that bronco?"

Wyatt might not have appreciated the tight expression on Lisa's face, but he wasn't about to let it stop him. Taking his time putting on his hat, he took a deep steady breath and said, "Do you still think I'm nice?"

Her chin came up and her lips parted in surprise. "Do you mean to tell me you rode that bronco because of me?"

"Maybe I was trying to make a point. Know what I think, Lisa?"

Suspicion narrowed her eyes.

"I think it worked. Do you still think I'm too nice to take you to dinner?"

He heard her sharp intake of breath and saw the softening in her gaze. Before his eyes, her expression changed and her resolve returned. "Wyatt, I don't think—"

"That's okay," he said, cutting off what was surely going to be another refusal. "There's no need to give me

your answer right now. Take all the time you need to think
it over.''

Without giving her a chance to get a word in edgewise,
he pulled at the brim of his hat, nodded at Melody, whose
eyes were as round as saucers, and strode away.

He didn't know why he looked over his shoulder, but
when he found Lisa watching him from ten paces away,
he turned around slowly and stared back at her. Her arms
were crossed, her chin set at a pensive angle, the mid-
August breeze trifling with her shoulder-length hair. She
didn't appear to know what to make of him, but he'd bet
his favorite horse that she wasn't thinking of him as a lily-
livered choirboy right now.

He would have liked to retrace his steps and kiss her all
over again, but he didn't want to give her the opportunity
to do to his ego what High Kicker had done to the seat of
his pants. So instead of doing what he wanted to do, he
cast her a smile she'd have a hard time deciphering, then
continued on his way.

He took his time removing Clayt's chaps, then hoisted
himself into the cab of his old pickup truck. The soreness
in his muscles was going to be worse tomorrow, but he
didn't care. That kiss Lisa had given him had been worth
a little pain, a little mud on his hat and sweat on his brow.

He wet his lips and tasted lipstick.

Oooo-eee. That kiss had definitely been worth it. The
memory alone made him wish he'd gone back for another.
But the next time he kissed her, he planned to do it in a
place that was a little quieter and a lot more private than
a bustling, bronc-stomping rodeo.

He'd promised to give her a little time. That shouldn't
be too difficult. He was a patient man, after all.

He turned the key in the ignition and pushed the lever
into first. The twilight sky took on a new duskiness as he

thought about the way she'd glided her hands around his neck, the way she'd sighed and melted against him. Breathing deeply, he wondered how much time he should give her. A day? A week?

The rapid thud of his pulse was his only answer.

Chapter Four

The porch swing creaked, insects hummed, and somewhere an engine backfired then faded away in the distance. Lisa pulled one leg up close to her body, then set the porch swing in motion all over again, her thoughts wandering along with the breeze blowing in from the plains.

The McKenzies, who lived next door, had called their brood in at nightfall. The little girl had skipped in happily, the boys following more slowly, complaining all the while. One by one, lights had come on all through the house. By ten o'clock the place had been dark again except one window that glimmered with the soft blue glow of a nightlight. Shortly thereafter, the other houses around her had grown dark, too.

This was a quiet street in a quiet town where families lived and worked and played, where voices rose, and laughter echoed, only to fade away to quieter sounds of padded footsteps and whispered good-nights. Lisa tried to tell herself she wasn't lonely. When that didn't work, she reminded herself that it was her own fault. Jillian and Luke had asked her along on their date; Mel had invited Lisa over to her place to watch a movie on her VCR. And DoraLee had issued a standing invitation to stop in at the Crazy Horse anytime she wanted.

But Jillian and Luke needed her on their date like a wagon needed a fifth wheel. And Lisa hadn't been in the mood for a movie, and she hadn't felt up to warding off the advances of the bachelors who frequented the town's only bar. Now she wished she'd done one or the other. At least then she wouldn't have been sitting all alone with nothing but her thoughts for company, wondering if her dreams would ever come true.

It wasn't as if her dreams were really so unusual. She didn't wish for riches or royalty or recognition. All she wanted was a home, a family, a man to love and a way to earn a living. This house on Elm Street she was renting was already starting to feel like a home. It was old, but sturdy. It wasn't picture-perfect, but at least the old-fashioned front porch with its peeling paint and weathered swing wasn't deceiving. She didn't like deception. In fact, there were a lot of things she didn't like. She didn't like dishonesty, or bullies who hurt other people. She didn't much care for bigots and snobs who sat in self-righteous judgment of others, either. No, she didn't like them, but she knew better than to try to change them. And she had to admit, every now and then, she enjoyed shocking them.

Nobody had been more shocked than she was when she'd realized she wanted children. It had happened four years ago when she'd picked her friend's daughter up from school. She'd taken one look at the children who were tossing footballs and playing tag, jumping rope and skipping hand in hand, and a wave of maternal instinct had washed over her with so much force tears had filled her eyes. Although she was a little nervous about her mothering abilities, the yearning hadn't gone away. From that day forward, she'd known she wanted to become a mother.

Timing, she'd learned, was everything. That was why it

had seemed almost too good to be true when she'd come across that article about a small town in South Dakota that was advertising for women. She'd read somewhere that every town bearing a name deserved a Western clothing store. She'd done her research, and after driving from Wisconsin to check out the village of Jasper Gulch, she'd known exactly what she wanted to do.

Tonight her dreams seemed as close as the stars in the sky and just as elusive, especially the one in which she found a man to love and who loved her in return. She didn't have many preconceived expectations when it came to men. Her future husband didn't have to be handsome or tall, rugged or rich, distinguished or powerful. But it would be nice if he was intelligent, and she'd love it if he could make her laugh. And it would be heaven if he could kiss half as well as Wyatt McCully.

She jerked to a stop so suddenly the swing creaked in protest. She thought she knew who Wyatt—the sheriff— was, but she hadn't been prepared for the man who'd ridden that bucking bronco tonight. Lisa wasn't blind. She knew how he looked in his sheriff uniform. But it wasn't until he'd stood before her in worn chaps and faded jeans that she'd realized he had the look, the style and, oh, yes, the moves to unsettle a feminine heart.

Headlights flickered as a truck turned the corner, then slowly pulled to a stop in front of her house. The engine was cut, the door pushed open. The next thing Lisa knew, the man she couldn't seem to get out of her mind was standing on the cracked sidewalk at the bottom of the porch steps as if it was the most natural thing in the world.

"Have you thought it over?" he asked.

It took her a few moments to realize he was referring to his invitation to dinner. She pushed the hair out of her eyes, lowered both feet to the floor and peered at him over the railing. "I thought you told me to take all the time I needed to think about it."

"I did."

"You call two hours all the time I need?"

"Two hours and ten minutes."

"Of course," she declared, "an extra ten minutes makes all the difference in the world."

"I thought you'd see it my way."

The porch light glinted off his hat, casting the top half of his face in shadow. She couldn't make out his eyes, but she could see the strong shape of his jaw, the shallow cleft in his chin and the firm line of his barely there smile.

Everything inside Lisa went completely still. It wasn't the first time this had happened, and she was beginning to believe it wouldn't be the last. She'd known there was something unique about this man the first time she'd seen him a month ago. She'd done everything in her power to steer clear of him in the days since. The only thing doing that had accomplished was to make the lure of his attraction even more powerful.

She tried to remind herself that this was Wyatt McCully, the local sheriff, the town's fair-haired favorite, who was perfect in every way. She tried to tell herself he wasn't the kind of man she was looking for. Her mind said the words, but her body didn't listen.

"Well?" he prodded.

"What am I going to do with you?" she countered.

He removed his hat and tilted his head. "You could invite me to sit down."

Lisa glanced at the dark houses all around, then at the man standing on her sidewalk, hat in hand. With a slight lift of her shoulders, she said, "Suit yourself."

Wyatt managed to walk up the stairs without groaning, but Lisa must have heard the hitch in his breathing when he dropped onto the swing, because she shook her head and said, "Serves you right for riding that bronco."

He gave her a sidelong glance, thinking it was just like a woman to tell a man "I told you so." She crossed her legs with a quiet swish, and he brought his left ankle up to rest on his right knee. Wyatt couldn't remember a time when he hadn't been aware of the differences between a man and a woman, but he'd never felt a stronger desire to know someone, what she thought and what she felt, on some deeper level.

"So?" he asked, searching for a place to begin. "What did you think of the rodeo?"

"It was nice."

He couldn't stop the disparaging sound coming from the back of his throat. "Nice? You thought the number-one spectator sport in South Dakota was nice? Gee, Lisa, could you be a little less enthusiastic?"

She stared straight ahead, smiling. "Next time I'll try to do better."

He pushed off with his foot, setting the swing in motion, wondering if she realized that she'd just implied there would be a next time. He would have liked to pin her down to a time and a place, but for now he decided to enjoy the easy conversation between them. They talked about the weather, the drought, the rain, and the clear, black sky. He told her about the fishing trip he took with his father when he was nine and his mother's blueberry pie, and she told him about the first time she met Jillian when they were both fifteen.

"If it hadn't been for Jillian, I don't know where I'd be today," Lisa said. "She took me home to her grandfather and introduced me to her next-door neighbors, then badgered me into staying. Ivy Pennington clucked over me like a mother hen, and although we're not blood related, Ivy, Jillian, Cori, and her daughter Allison, are more like family than my mother and father ever were."

Wyatt didn't think he'd ever heard so much loyalty and honest affection in another person's voice. Lisa obviously cared a great deal about her friends. Settling his shoulders more comfortably against the back of the swing, he said,

"It couldn't have been easy for you and Jillian to leave them behind."

"Things have a way of changing. Cori just got married, and Allison is growing up. Coming here seemed like the right thing to do, and now seems like the right time to do it. I've always been able to adapt to change. Actually I consider it one of my strengths, but I've never lived in a place like this. Madison, Wisconsin, isn't exactly a bustling metropolis, but I'm still amazed by the utter silence out here. Have the people of Jasper Gulch always rolled up the sidewalks at nine o'clock?"

"It's a village ordinance."

Lisa laughed, the sound seeping into his chest, causing his breathing to deepen and his voice to drop in volume. "Would you say you like it so far?" he asked.

He sensed, more than saw, her shrug. "The men are friendly, but most of the women are reserved. And I'm pretty sure Isabell Pruitt hates me."

"Isabell hates everybody."

That got her attention. "She does?"

Wyatt nodded. "There isn't a living soul in Jasper Gulch who hasn't been on the receiving end of that woman's pointed finger and wagging tongue. Luke and Clayt used to call her Olive Oyl. Still do if they know she's listening."

"Oh, Wyatt, you're so bad."

"That's what I've been trying to tell you."

She turned her head slowly and looked into his eyes. Wyatt wondered how a man was supposed to keep from getting lost in the expression in those clear, dark eyes. Emotions stirred inside him, and his gaze dropped to her mouth. Her lips parted, in surprise or anticipation, he couldn't be sure. His thoughts slowed, his blood thickening into need.

She dragged her gaze away from his and turned her

head, the movement putting an end to his kiss before it started. "It's getting late."

She rose suddenly and strode to the railing. Wyatt followed more slowly, saying, "That sounded a little like 'There's no hurry but here's your hat.' Are you trying to get rid of me, Lisa?"

When she didn't answer, he went down one step, so that their eyes were on the same level. "Now do you think you've had long enough to think about going someplace, anyplace, with me?"

Staring into his eyes, she said, "All the time in the world isn't going to change the fact that I'm not the kind of woman you're looking for."

He barely moved as he said, "And what kind of woman is that?"

"Oh, someone sweet and gentle and nice, someone who had a normal childhood. Someone whose father has never been in prison, and who has the kind of mother a person could send cards to on special occasions. Someone who hasn't lived in deserted warehouses, and who hasn't stolen to eat."

The porch light cast a yellow glow over her skin, giving her hair a dark luster and her eyes a glimmer every bit as moving as tears. Staring into those eyes, a few things about Lisa Markman were becoming clear. He'd thought the reason she was fighting her feelings with everything she had was because of the way she perceived him. Now he realized it had as much to do with the way she perceived herself. She thought he was nice. And she thought she wasn't.

He studied her thoughtfully for a moment, certain she could hear the pounding of his heart. Sure enough, her head came up and her chin jutted out and she said, "I don't like what you're thinking."

"How do you know what I'm thinking?"

"Believe me. I know."

"Admit it, Lisa. You like me."

She eyed him with a calculating expression that had probably put a lot of men off, then quietly said, "For a nice guy, you aren't too bad."

He went down another step and fought back a smile. "You aren't so bad yourself. Good night, Lisa."

Lisa stared at Wyatt in amazement. She mumbled something that passed for goodbye, then stood statue still, watching him walk away. He had a smooth gate, a long stride and a masculine swagger that seemed at odds with the gentlemanly way he put on his hat.

She stayed where she was long after the engine rumbled to life and the truck's red taillights disappeared around the corner. Tipping her head back, she looked at the stars in the sky, then at the lone street lamp at the end of the block. The breeze fluttered through her hair, raising goose bumps on her arms. She'd once read that the Lakota Indians who used to roam the plains had believed that the wind had special powers, and if you listened hard enough you could hear it talking, and you'd never be alone. Listening to the sounds the wind made as it pushed through the leaves high in the trees, she almost believed it was true. It reminded her of the low, husky tone of Wyatt's voice when he'd said, *You aren't so bad yourself.*

The man wasn't a poet, but he definitely had a way with words. He had a way of surprising her, too, and of catching her off guard. But there was more to him than that, more, even, than a cowboy swagger and a gentlemanly disposition. He was nice, but he also brought out her lightning-quick reflexes.

Feeling strangely lighthearted, she turned around and headed inside. The screen door creaked when she opened it and bounced twice when it closed behind her. She left the porch light on for Jillian, then went about the business of getting ready for bed. The clock struck midnight while she was crawling between her smooth sheets. Yawning, she closed her eyes and smiled into her pillow. Tomorrow was another day, and for the first time in weeks, she could hardly wait for it to arrive.

"Hopefully I'll find a wedding gown on Saturday," Jillian said, her voice slightly muffled by the heavy curtain covering the dressing room doorway. "If I don't find one in Rapid City, I'm going to have to go all the way to Aberdeen, and honestly, I just don't know when I'll find the time."

"We'll find the perfect gown," Lisa said, removing a pin from a little boy's Western shirt on the other side of the store.

"Finding a dress is only the beginning. There's just so much to do. Luke, bless his heart, is absolutely no help whatsoever. If he had his way, the wedding would be tomorrow. Tomorrow! How in the world could I possibly plan a wedding by tomorrow? I don't even know how I'm going to get everything done in a month."

The curtain fluttered here and moved there as Jillian bumped it with her elbow and grazed it with her knee. Removing the last stack of children's blue jeans from the carton, Lisa grinned to herself. Her best friend was normally cool, calm and collected. But that was before Luke Carson had swept her off her feet.

Lisa rushed past the dressing rooms, her arms piled high with new merchandise. Jillian talked on, and Lisa bustled from one end of the store to the other.

"Well?" Jillian asked a few minutes later. "What do you think?"

Checking the sign above a shelf, Lisa said, "I think it's lovely."

"Thanks. But Lisa?"

"Hmm?" she asked absently.

"Your compliment would probably be more effective if you actually looked at me before you said it."

Lisa turned slowly, a smile on her face even before she saw the sardonic lift of Jillian's chin. "You could be right. But honestly, Jillian, with the glow you've been wearing lately, you'd look great in men's overalls."

Turning this way and that in front of the three-sided mirror, Jillian said, "Now you sound like Luke. But really, these new skirts are beautiful. And when did you decide to stock bras, slips and panties?"

Lisa pushed her hair out of her eyes then bent down to retrieve a hanger. "I'm hoping to draw in the women in town. Everybody wears underwear, right?" Thinking about Big Rose and Donna Faye, two women she'd met the very first time she ran away, Lisa skewed her mouth to one side and said, "Well, almost everybody."

Jillian went back into the dressing room, and Lisa breathed a sigh of relief. She'd been asleep when Jillian came in last night, and had slipped out of the house before she got up this morning. It wasn't as if Lisa was avoiding her best friend. It was just that she'd wakened at the break of dawn, filled with vitality and renewed enthusiasm. She had a million things to do today, and she was only halfway through her list. She couldn't help it if her pep and vigor kept Jillian from mentioning the kiss Wyatt had given her at the rodeo last night, but she could thank her lucky stars.

She was arranging bras and panties on a glass shelf when Jillian opened the curtain and stepped out of the dressing room wearing her own clothes. "Lisa," she said, sashaying closer. "There's something I want to say."

Hesitating, Lisa measured the expression in Jillian's wide blue eyes. "Yes?"

"It's good to see the sparkle in your eyes again."

Lisa relaxed. "You know what Ivy always says. 'When the going gets tough, the tough get going.'"

Jillian turned toward the door. "Yes, that sounds like Ivy, and that reminds me, I'm expecting a call from her at noon, and I still have to stop by Luke's office before going

home, so I'd better go. I'll see you at supper tonight.
Maybe then you'll be ready to tell me if that kiss Wyatt
McCully collected after riding that bronco last night has
anything to do with your sudden lively mood."

Lisa swung around, and Jillian laughed, ducking out the
open door a split second before the item sailing through
the air could hit its mark. With a shake of her head, Lisa
turned back to her task, wondering why she'd ever let Jillian badger her into going home with her all those years
ago.

The thud of footsteps near the doorway drew her around
in time to see Wyatt lean over to pick something up from
the floor. Straightening, he held up his hand, a dark purple
bra dangling from his fingers. "Are you giving away door
prizes, Lisa?"

She was momentarily speechless, and that didn't happen
very often. She couldn't even take any satisfaction in the
fact that bending over hadn't appeared to be easy for him.
Marching toward him, she snatched the garment from his
hand. "A word of advice, Wyatt," she said, raising her
voice since she knew Jillian was still within hearing range.
"Never underestimate a redhead."

"My hair is not red." The door clicked shut on anything
else Jillian might have said.

Now that Wyatt's eyes had adjusted to the dim interior,
he looked around. This wasn't the first time he'd been
inside the new Jasper Gulch Clothing Store, nor was it the
first time he'd witnessed the quirky little moments of argument and humor that made up Lisa and Jillian's friendship. Lisa was still shaking her head, but there was no real
ire in her eyes or in her voice when she said, "Luke's in
big trouble."

Striding to the center of the store, Wyatt said, "Then
you don't know Luke the way I do. Whatever trouble he's
in, he'll give back to Jillian one hundred fold."

He turned slowly, his eyes trained on Lisa. She was

looking at him, her dark hair grazing her eyes, the rest hanging in a graceful curve to her shoulders. She was wearing a long denim skirt that buttoned up one side and a sleeveless white shirt complete with fringe and silver studs. If he spent more time than he should have staring at lush curves underneath, he couldn't help it. No woman had ever made Western clothing look so good.

As if she suddenly became aware of the silence stretching between them, she asked, "Did you stop by to do a little shopping?"

Wyatt held up one hand and shook his head. "I'm afraid I rate shopping right up there with smashing my thumb in a car door."

Going back to her task, she said, "No wonder business is so slow. If you're not here to shop, what can I do for you, Wyatt?"

He stared at her down-turned eyes, thinking, Now there's a question. He could name a hundred things she could do for him, to him, with him. One glance out the window at the people who were out and about on the village Main Street reminded him that this wasn't exactly a private setting. Since he really was here on official business, he reined in his wayward thoughts and said, "I just came from a wild-goose chase down in Draper, and I wanted to talk to you about your car."

"My car is down in Draper?"

"I didn't find your car, but I do have a few questions I'd like to ask you." Strolling to a display of men's blue jeans, he said, "Nice place."

"I think so."

His back was to her, but he could tell by her voice that she was coming closer. "Are you sure I can't help you find something?" she asked.

He turned slowly and looked directly into her eyes. "I know exactly what I want."

Lisa wet her lips, but there wasn't much she could do

about the slow, smooth slide her heart took into her stomach. It had happened after he'd kissed her last night, and again when he'd told her she wasn't so bad herself. The first time it had happened, she'd blamed it on the beat of horses hooves, the cheer of the crowd and the sight of Wyatt in chaps and spurs. The second time she'd attributed it to loneliness. This time she couldn't find any excuse for the softening sensation deep inside.

Pulling her thoughts together, she said, "Did you get a lead on my car?"

He nodded. "I received an anonymous tip over the phone this morning. The caller said he'd seen a red car with Wisconsin plates in Draper, so I drove on down and asked around. Draper is even smaller than Jasper Gulch. If a red car passed through there, the old men sitting in front of Smitty's General Store would have noticed."

"Has anyone seen it?" she asked.

Wyatt shook his head. "I don't think your car was ever in Draper."

"Why would somebody say it had been?"

"I don't know. We had a bad connection, and the voice was so muffled and garbled I couldn't place it. But there was still something familiar about it."

"Then you think somebody right here in Jasper Gulch took my car?"

He nodded. "There are cars and trucks parked in every driveway on every street in Jasper Gulch. Half of them are newer than yours, and most of them have the keys in the ignition. Yet this person took yours."

Lisa studied Wyatt thoughtfully. He wasn't wearing his hat today. Without it, she could see the tiny lines beside his eyes and the deeper one creasing his cheek. She remembered how indignant he'd looked yesterday when he'd told her he didn't spend all his time rescuing kittens out of trees. Today his expression was calculating and intense, and left little doubt that he was capable of handling much more serious situations.

Striding closer, she asked, "Do you have any idea who took my car or why?"

"Everybody I see has their own two-bit theory. Isabell Pruitt thinks it's the work of the devil. Boomer Brown is convinced a ring of car thieves has moved into the area."

"But you don't agree with either of those theories."

The shake of his head was almost imperceptible, but the sheen of purpose in his eyes might as well have been carved in stone. "I think it's something a lot simpler than that."

"What could be more simple than a ring of car thieves?"

"There hasn't been another car reported stolen in a sixty-five-mile radius all year. If this was anyplace else, I'd say teenagers might have been responsible. I'm not saying the local teenagers *couldn't* have done it, but I don't think this was a teenage prank."

"Then what was it?" she asked, more curious than ever.

Staring directly into her eyes, he said, "I think it's more likely to have been one of the bachelors vying for your attention."

The deep timbre of Wyatt's voice held Lisa perfectly still. His voice was always filled with intensity, but today it was so low and dark and clear she could practically feel the vibration on her skin.

"One of the Jasper Gents?" she asked incredulously.

He nodded slowly. "Can you think of anybody who's been hanging around more since it happened?"

"There's you."

Lisa came to her senses with a start, her gaze climbing to his. The smile faded from his face, only to be replaced by a much more powerful expression. "Do you think I took your car, Lisa?"

She shook her head.

"Why not?" he asked.

"Because you're as honest as the day is long." This time, she couldn't make it sound like a bad thing.

He smiled, and she swallowed, searching frantically for something else to say. The bell over the door jingled. Lisa turned her head as if in slow motion, her vision clearing the instant she saw Louetta Graham enter the store.

The other woman took a few steps, then stopped in her tracks. She mumbled a greeting, then blushed to the roots of her drab brown hair. "Pardon me. I didn't know you had company."

Hurrying toward the shy woman, Lisa said, "Sheriff McCully isn't company, Louetta. He's here on business."

Wyatt took a few steps toward her. "It's true, Louetta. Lisa and I were just talking about her stolen car."

Louetta's gaze darted from Wyatt to Lisa, then to the toes of her sensible shoes. "Oh, I see. Well, if anybody can get your car back for you, Lisa, Wyatt can. Um, I just remembered there's something else I have to do."

She hurried out of the store so fast her long, starched skirt fluttered in her wake. Staring at the place she'd been, Lisa said, "That was strange."

"Not for Louetta."

Ignoring Wyatt's comment, Lisa continued to think out loud. "She's been coming in every day at exactly eleven-thirty for a week, and I've never seen her this tongue-tied."

"I've never seen her any other way."

Lisa glanced sideways at Wyatt, then at the bell over the door. "I think I know why she left so suddenly. I think she likes you."

"Not the way you mean."

She was so surprised by the depth of authority in Wyatt's voice that she found herself face-to-face with him without realizing she'd moved. "Then you don't think she has a crush on you?" she sputtered.

He shook his head one time. "Louetta Graham is painfully shy, but she isn't interested in me."

"How can you be so sure?"

His gaze narrowed in on hers as he said, "Because a man can tell when a woman is interested."

Lisa swallowed. "He can?"

Wyatt nodded, and she swallowed all over again.

"Aren't you going to ask how I can tell?" he said, taking a step closer.

"I'm waiting for something."

He took another step, openly studying her. "What could you possibly be waiting for?"

"For hell to freeze over."

Wyatt stopped in his tracks, his entire face sliding into a grin. Damn, he liked it when she raised her chin at that haughty angle and spoke in that insolent, high-handed tone of voice. Angling her his best killer smile, he said, "Then you're not blinded by my brains and good looks?"

Nobody but Lisa could have pulled off such an indignant *harrumph*. She placed her hands on her hips and jutted out her chin. "Thank goodness it hasn't gone to your head."

He didn't know how long he stood there without moving, adrenaline and pure male appreciation surging through him. He'd thought about Lisa long after he'd gone to bed last night. Somewhere around two a.m., he'd reached a decision. No more being Mr. Nice Guy. It was time to call in the big guns. It was time to turn up the heat and turn on the charm. Wyatt McCully was going to make this woman his if he had to break the law to do it.

Strolling closer, he said, "I hate to sound like a broken record, but about that dinner I mentioned."

Holding her ground and his gaze, she said, "What about it?"

"I want to spend time with you. Alone. Man to woman.

If you don't accept peacefully, I might be forced to arrest you.''

Lisa knew she should try to put an end to this, here and now, but her gaze strayed to the masculine curve of his mouth, her mind conjuring up an image of him standing before her in chaps, spurs and rodeo dust. For reasons she didn't fully understand, she didn't want to tell him no.

"Come on, Lisa, what do you say?''

"I can't, Wyatt.''

"What do you mean you can't?''

She'd responded to him physically the first time she'd seen him a month ago. The baffled expression on his face right now brought an entirely different tug on her insides. Lisa Markman had never been a coward. She'd never run from the truth. And the truth was she liked this man. It just so happened that she always tried to give the people she liked honest answers. With her courage and determination like a rock inside her, she looked straight into his eyes and said, "I can't have dinner with you tonight because I'm working at the diner.''

"You're moonlighting?''

Nodding, she tried to explain. "I did a lot of thinking after you left last night. You might even say I took stock of my situation and came up with a new plan. I read that it can take up to five years to get a business off the ground. It didn't take that long for the catering business I started back in Madison to climb out of the red, but until the store starts showing a profit, it looks as if I'm going to be putting my waitressing skills to use.''

He stood motionless a few feet from her. "I see. And what did you decide to do about me?''

Staring into his golden brown eyes, Lisa thought it was no wonder she hadn't been able to get him out of her mind. She'd tried fighting her feelings, and she'd tried ignoring them. Maybe it was time she faced them. Completely aware of the tingling in the pit of her stomach, she squared her shoulders and said, "Mel usually closes the diner around seven. You could stop by then."

He didn't smile, and for a long time he didn't move. Finally he turned on his heel and strode to the door. With one hand on the doorknob, he glanced over his shoulder and said, "Seven o'clock? I'll see you then."

Chapter Five

Voices rose and fell, hearty guffaws mingling with the
sound of clattering forks and rattling saucers. Wyatt took
a sip of his coffee and looked around him at the people
who'd gathered in the town's only restaurant. Thursdays
were usually relatively slow in Mel's Diner. Tonight every
one of the ten tables and eight booths were occupied. Although his sister was a darned good cook, Wyatt didn't
believe for a second that the bachelors of Jasper Gulch had
come in for Mel's pepper steak and hash browns.

The diner wasn't new and it certainly wasn't fancy. It
was the kind of place where a cowboy could eat his entire
meal without taking off his hat. Oddly enough, the hat
racks on both sides of the door were full tonight. The local
bachelors' sudden show of good manners had nothing to
do with the fact that the diner seemed to have acquired an
astonishing amount of class and atmosphere. The new
waitress was responsible for that.

"Hey, Lisa! Could you give me a refill when you get a
minute?" Neil Anderson called.

"Me, too," his brother Ned added.

"And I could use a slice of Mel's apple pie," the youngest Anderson brother declared.

"But there's no hurry," all three of them said at the same time.

Clayt practically snorted. "Those boys are about as subtle as a thunderstorm."

Wyatt didn't say anything, but neither of the Carson brothers appeared ready to drop the subject. Luke shook his head and made a disparaging sound before saying, "I admit that Neil's pretty darned good on the banjo, and Ned and Norbert aren't half-bad on the guitar. I might even go so far as to say that when the three of them harmonize, they sound a little like Garth, himself. But if they know the first thing about impressing a woman, I'll be Jasper Gulch's next preacher."

"Amen to that," Clayt said under his breath.

The thought of Luke Carson as a preacher made Wyatt laugh out loud. He slurped the last of his coffee and glanced up at the men at his table who had suddenly gone as quiet as church mice. Cletus was wearing his usual suspenders, Luke and Clayt their usual scowls. All of them were looking at him as if he'd grown an extra nose.

"What?" he asked, lowering his empty cup to the table.

"It just occurred to me," Clayt said, his voice ominously low, "that you don't appear the least bit put out by the way these boys are flirting with the woman you've had your eye on since the moment she set foot in Jasper Gulch."

"Yeah," Luke agreed. "Clayt told me about the bucking bronc you rode at the rodeo last night, and by now everybody's heard about the kiss Lisa gave you for your trouble. I was fit to be tied last month when the local boys started bringing every stray cat and dog they could get their hands on into the animal clinic just to get closer to Jillian. You might be ten times more patient than Clayt and me, but these boys would try the patience of a saint, and nobody has that much patience. Not even you.''

Wyatt glanced at his grandfather for moral support and was rewarded with a halfhearted shrug. So much for Cletus coming to his rescue. The truth of the matter was Wyatt didn't see how he could argue with Carson logic, not when Lisa had told him to stop by the diner around seven, and he'd moseyed in shortly after five-thirty. But before he could say as much, deep, sultry laughter drew his gaze to the other side of the room, and Wyatt forgot what he'd been going to say.

Lisa was wearing the same denim skirt and sleeveless shirt she'd had on when he'd dropped in on her at the store earlier. He'd never thought of an apron as sexy attire, but the way the well-worn scrap of cloth was tied around her waist and hugged her hips and the lush curves of her breasts made him rethink his former opinion. She'd fastened her hair on top of her head with a bright blue clip. Wispy tendrils had come loose, twining down her neck and around her face.

He'd been watching her for more than an hour and had seen her flit from one end of the diner to the other wielding a coffee carafe and balancing a tray. She must have an incredible memory, because she took orders without writing them down. As far as he could tell, she hadn't mixed up anybody's supper, not even Grover Andrews's, and he'd changed his mind three times.

''Is there a reason—other than the scenery—that you're sitting here with a knowing grin on your face?'' Clayt groused.

Wyatt pulled his gaze from the other side of the room and found Clayt, Luke and Cletus watching him expectantly. ''Well?'' Luke prodded.

Running a hand over his chin, Wyatt gave each man a long look, then quietly said, ''I admit that I'm not thrilled with the way the local boys keep ogling Lisa's chest, and the first time one of the bachelors asked her out tonight, I sat up a little straighter, that's for sure.''

"But it doesn't bother you anymore?" Luke asked.

Wyatt shrugged. "She's turned down two more invitations since then. And I know why."

The other three men all leaned ahead in their chairs, their elbows on the table, their heads cocked at a better angle to hear. "Well?" Clayt sputtered. "Are you going to tell us why?"

"Because she isn't interested in them. She's interested in me."

"How do you know?"

Wyatt slanted Clayt a sardonic look. Little by little, smiles found their way to Clayt's, Luke's and Cletus's faces. One by one, they all rose to their feet. The Carson brothers slapped Wyatt on the back, and Cletus grinned from ear to ear as if the credit was all his.

"No wonder you're sittin' there like the cat who swallowed the canary whole," Cletus declared. To Clayt and Luke, he said, "Come on, you two, maybe if we get out of here, the other boys will follow suit and Wyatt will be able to steal the new waitress away for a few hours."

Smiling, too, Luke nodded and said, "It's time I was leaving anyway. Jillian and I have a date."

Clayt said, "And I have to pick Haley up from Jeremy Everts's house. I think she's finally made a friend. Good luck, Wyatt."

Wyatt didn't say anything, but anticipation strummed through him just the same. Luck? He wasn't planning to rely on luck. He was going to rely on instinct, and the honest-to-goodness attraction that had been pulsing through him like a blip of radar since the first moment he'd laid eyes on Lisa Markman.

"Thanks," Lisa called, pocketing a tip from one of the local bachelors.

"Have a nice night," the man called from the door.

After giving him her famous wink, she turned around again and surveyed the room. The Anderson brothers were finishing up their pie at a table in the middle of the diner. Boomer Brown was polishing off the last of his hot fudge sundae across the booth from Jason Tucker, who was shoveling his supper into his mouth as if it were his last meal. And Wyatt was pretending to drink a cup of coffee, watching her every move from a table in one corner.

He nodded and smiled. She turned back to her tasks, that grin he gave her dallying around the edges of her mind for a long time. The same thing had happened after he'd left her store that morning. She'd done a lot of thinking since then, and while she wasn't denying the pull of attraction she felt every time she saw him, she still didn't believe Wyatt was the right man for her, and vice versa. They were complete opposites.

She'd once kicked a policeman in the shins to escape his clutches, and Wyatt had never been in any real trouble in his life. He came from a stable home, and she just plain didn't. Her past was riddled with sordid details while his reputation was squeaky clean.

Lisa had always been a woman of her word, and she wasn't about to change now. But she was trying to give him one more chance to see her the way she really was.

"Hey, Lisa!" Jason Tucker mumbled around a mouthful of mashed potatoes. "Boomer and I have a little wager going. I say you weigh a hundred and twenty-five, but Boomer says you couldn't weigh a pound over one eighteen."

Balancing a tray of dishes on one hip, she sashayed closer. "Jason," she said, her voice husky with laughter, "the only man who's ever gotten away with guessing my weight was Big Bubba, one of the carnies I met the week I ran the kiddie cars at the Indianapolis Free Fair. He was a brute of a man with a handlebar mustache and only one good eye, but he could guess a person's weight within a pound one way or the other. According to Bertha, who ran the Ferris wheel, that's how he lost his right eye.''

The Anderson brothers laughed in the background. Giving Boomer a broad wink, she said, ''And you! If you ever want to give up the glitter and glamour of a rancher's life, you could take over Big Bubba's job.''

''Shoot.'' Jason stopped shoveling food into his mouth and handed Boomer a five dollar bill. Turning to Lisa, he said, ''Wanna go for a drive with me when you get off work?''

''That's a tempting offer,'' she said, ''but I'm afraid I won't have much time for late-night drives for a while.''

''Why is that?'' one of the Anderson brothers called.

Continuing to place used dishes on the tray, she said, ''Until business picks up in the store, I'm going to be working evenings and weekends for Melody and Dora-Lee.''

The three brothers all stood. One of them, she thought his name was Neil, said, ''Business isn't so good?''

She shook her head. ''Maybe I should advertise.''

Jason piped up and said, ''Far as I'm concerned, the way you look in your store's clothes is advertisement enough.''

Boomer shrugged his massive shoulders. ''I'm afraid folks out here aren't much for shopping, Lisa, but if you really want to boost your sales, you oughta sell a kiss with every pair of blue jeans.''

''Yeah,'' one of the other men insisted. ''That would bring in an extra sixty-one dollars. Make that sixty-two, on account'a I'd buy two.''

Wyatt found his feet slowly. Keeping his eyes trained on Lisa, he reached into his pocket and dropped a bill onto the table, her sultry laugh working over him in waves. She bid the other diners goodbye, telling them they were brilliant, and that she'd keep their suggestion in mind. Wyatt doubted that any of them were aware they'd been effectively ushered out of the room.

Lisa may have been sultry and warm and more than a little brash, but she treated the bachelors with equal parts humor and respect. She had them eating out of her hand, and they all knew it. She could turn a man down without hurting his feelings, every rejoinder accompanied with a wink, a laugh and a genuine smile. The woman was amazing. What was even more amazing was the way his heart beat with the knowledge.

Pans clanked in the kitchen; Lisa and Wyatt both turned toward the sound, their gazes meeting all over again.

"It isn't going to work, you know," he said, striding closer.

Lisa distributed her weight to one foot, her hands settling to her hips. Glancing at the only remaining hat on the rack by the door, she said, "I know. Those men wouldn't really pay good money for a kiss. A kiss *is* just a kiss, after all."

"A kiss is *not* just a kiss."

The deep, husky tone of Wyatt's voice replaced the smile on her mouth with something that felt deeper, darker and much more sensuous. "It isn't?"

He shook his head. "A kiss is instinctive, unforgettable. At least yours was."

"It was?" Lisa wondered when she'd become an idiot. She was pretty sure she'd been perfectly sane a few minutes ago. But now she couldn't even put two thoughts together. All because Wyatt was looking at her, his eyes trained on her mouth.

"Yes, it was," he said, his voice barely more than a husky whisper, "but I wasn't talking about a kiss, when I said it wasn't going to work. Did you really think the fact that you once worked at a traveling carnival would scare me away?"

She couldn't control the telltale lift of her eyebrows, but

she did have the presence of mind to silently commend Wyatt for being so astute. Feeling her wits rejuvenate, she angled him a look she'd perfected years ago. "Don't say I didn't warn you."

"I promise I'll never say that." He reached behind her, deftly untying her apron strings. Holding her still with his steady gaze, he tossed the apron to a chair and said, "What do you say we get out of here?"

"I really should help Mel clean up."

Wyatt turned toward the kitchen, a sense of purpose lengthening his stride. He poked his head inside the doorway and called, "Everyone's gone, Mel. I'm taking Lisa home."

The door swished shut on his sister's gaping stare. He turned on his heel and strode back to the dining room, not stopping until he was directly in front of Lisa. "Well? What are we waiting for?"

She stood motionless, her eyes round, her lips parted slightly. And then, in one lithe movement, she spun around and said, "I like your style, McCully."

Wyatt strode to her side, stopping at the door only long enough to reach for his hat.

"See that wide spot in the creek?"

Looking out the side window, Lisa would have nodded even if Wyatt's old pickup truck hadn't bounced into another chuckhole and slowly crawled out the other side.

"That's the swimming hole where Clayt, Luke and I went skinning-dipping one hot Fourth of July. Isabell Pruitt's mother caught us. Oooo-eee. She was fit to be tied."

Lisa smiled at the hint of boastfulness in Wyatt's voice. They'd been driving for more than two hours, bumping over every pothole on every back road they'd encountered. He'd shown her the small clapboard structure that had once been used as the old Grange Hall, and the one-room schoolhouse where he'd attended the first grade. The windows and doors on the old brick building were boarded up now, but as she listened to the stories Wyatt wove, she could practically see the old seesaws and the baseball games being played during recess.

History had always fascinated her. She'd read about the gulch near Garretson that Jesse James had once jumped to escape a posse, and the man known as Crooked Nose Jack who'd gunned down Wild Bill Hickok in a saloon in Deadwood on the other side of the state. South Dakota was steeped in folklore of famous brawls and interesting people. To hear Wyatt tell it, Jasper Gulch was no exception.

"Jasper Carson, Luke and Clayt's great-great-grandfather, founded the town more than a hundred years ago. According to legend, Jasper came to this area by way of the Black Hills. He had a little gold in his pockets and a widow he'd won in a poker game at his side.

"The Widow Barnes wasn't too happy about her situation. According to a journal old Jasper kept, she didn't utter a single word to him during the entire ride from Lead. By the time he'd reached the Bad River, he was mighty tired of talking to himself, and mighty anxious to steal a kiss from Abigail. So he made a little wager with his new bride. He bet her that he could cross the river without getting his boots wet. If he lost, she could leave, taking all the gold in his pockets with her. But if he won, she'd have to do three things. Talk to him, kiss him and promise to stay."

For a moment Wyatt's voice faded to a hushed stillness. They'd reached the curb in front of Lisa's house. The sun had gone down an hour ago, the only light inside the truck coming from the illumination on the dash. Staring at his dark profile, Lisa said, "Did Abigail take the bet?"

Wyatt opened the door, throwing the dim overhead light on. "Oh, she took the bet, all right. She probably felt pretty smug staring at the swift current in that river. I imagine her smugness turned to dismay when Jasper unhooked the horse from the wagon, led him down the river bank, and climbed on. When the water got deep enough for the horse to swim, Jasper stood on the horse's back until he made it to the other side. Bone-dry.''

Wyatt strode around the truck and opened her door. Another time Lisa would have commented on the gentlemanly gesture, but tonight, her curiosity got the best of her. Sliding her feet to the ground, she said, "Did Abigail keep her end of the bargain?"

"Sometime I'll show you the crumbled remains of the fireplace in the first shanty they built on the Carson Ranch.''

"Did she talk to him after that?" Lisa asked.

"Yelled her first two words across the river before Jasper had dismounted.''

Stepping onto the cracked sidewalk in front of her house, Lisa said, "Wouldn't you love to know what she said?''

"It's in Jasper's journal, but I can't repeat it in front of a lady.''

Lisa laughed out loud. "What about the kiss?"

Wyatt hiked his boot onto the bottom porch step and said, "Jasper swam back across the river to collect that. Men have been known to do some pretty incredible things for a kiss.''

His voice stopped Lisa on the top step. She'd seen firsthand what Wyatt would do for a kiss, and was reminded of it all over again every time she caught sight of his little limp. He'd ridden a wild horse. And she'd kissed him. No matter how many times she tried to tell herself there hadn't been anything unique about that kiss, she remained unconvinced.

Strange things had been happening inside her ever since. Dreamy things, feminine things, whispery, shimmery, starry-eyed things. Wyatt could make her smile. Heck, he could make her feel like humming, and Lisa Markman rarely hummed. She was used to men's gazes straying below her shoulders. She'd caught Wyatt staring a time or two, but she couldn't shake the feeling that there were things he liked about her other than her bra size. It was strange, but when she was with him, she didn't feel lonely.

She glanced at her own dark windows, then turned and stared down into Wyatt's dark eyes. "Would you like to come in for a little while?"

He looked up at her through half-closed lids, then took the remaining steps two at a time.

Wyatt settled his back more comfortably against the old refrigerator behind him. Lisa was standing a few feet away, arms and ankles crossed, her hips resting against the counter.

"Well?" she said. "Now that you've had the grand tour, what do you think of the place?"

He'd been in this house back when Wilbur and Lucille Jacobs had lived here before they retired to Arizona. The house hadn't changed much, structurally at least. The cabinets were still old and the floors were still uneven.

Cletus always said you could tell a lot about a person by stepping into his house. Wyatt supposed that was true enough. Lisa's furniture had probably been new once, but not in the past two decades. Still, it was functional and comfortable. And the brightly colored rugs and throw pillows and the antique lamp with the red fringe next to the sofa had flair written all over them.

He hadn't been surprised when she'd reached for the bowl of lemons on her counter and made lemonade from scratch. But if he'd expected Lisa to be asleep on her feet after working all day in her store then handling the supper crowd at the diner, she'd proven him wrong. She'd shown him through her house, her hands and feet in a constant flutter of movement, a story behind every chair, bookcase and potted plant. Wyatt found himself wishing she'd turn that kind of energy loose on him. His pulse quickened from the thought alone, spreading heat from his head to his toes.

Evidently misinterpreting his silence, she said, "Don't worry, Sheriff, the old adage 'If you can't say something nice don't say anything at all' doesn't apply to me. I can take the truth."

Wyatt took his time crossing his ankles, the action doing little to relieve the need building inside him. "The truth?" he said quietly. "In that case, I think your house is almost as nice as you are."

Her eyes widened in surprise, then narrowed in speculation. "I'm not sure how to take that."

He laughed in spite of his resolve not to. "You sound like a guy I met in boot camp."

Her chin came around with a jerk, the wisps of hair that had escaped the clasp on top of her head fluttering around her neck. "You were in the army?"

He lowered his chin and his voice. "Did you think you were the only person with secrets in your past?"

"We're not talking about me. What made you decide to join the army?"

Wyatt hadn't planned to talk about this, but now that he'd brought it up, he didn't see any way around it. Trying to maintain an even tone of voice, he began. "I graduated from high school right on schedule. Suddenly, there I was without a clue what to do with the rest of my life. My parents were gone, and my grandfather was talking about selling off part of the ranch. He was getting older, and I think he knew that ranching wasn't in my blood. So one day I decided to visit Luke at college. Instead of coming back to South Dakota, I joined the army."

Lisa had a feeling he was leaving a lot out, but he'd hit enough high spots for her to get the general picture. This was something she'd never considered. She knew that

Luke Carson had left Jasper Gulch to attend Michigan State University, but for some reason, she'd assumed that Wyatt was the type of man who never would have wanted to leave his hometown. Staring at the tense line of his jaw, she said, "What did Cletus say about your leaving?"

"I'd been talking about it for weeks. He wasn't surprised."

She spun away to the small table, then stood with her hands on the back of one of her painted kitchen chairs. "Did you like it?" she asked.

"The army?" He shrugged. "I wouldn't recommend it to everybody. In fact, I experienced the single most embarrassing moment of my life my first day there, but I met some interesting people. And I grew up. By the time I'd put in my three years, I knew I'd seen enough army bases and had eaten enough cafeteria food to last a lifetime. I wanted to come home. Lately I've been mighty glad I did."

Lisa could tell by the expression in his eyes that he was including her arrival in Jasper Gulch in his reasons for being glad. She tried to square her shoulders against his allure. But then he smiled, deepening a crease in one lean cheek. Her eyelids lowered, her breath stuck in her throat, and she smiled in return.

Tucking a strand of hair behind her ear, she said, "Would you tell me something, Wyatt?"

"Anything you want to know."

"What, exactly, was the most embarrassing moment you mentioned?"

Wyatt cringed. He hadn't thought about any of this in years, and he'd never told another living soul about that day when he'd been eighteen. Leave it to Lisa to ask him about it now. Running a hand through his hair, he considered making something up. One look at the curiosity in her wide, brown eyes, and he couldn't lie.

Heaving a huge sigh, he said, "I was in a room full of

other new recruits. We'd taken the written exam and had had our eyes and ears tested. From there, we were instructed to remove everything except our shoes. I wasn't thrilled with the orders, but I did as I was told and got in line.

"I'd had physicals before, and I knew what to expect. I *hadn't* expected the officers in charge to break out laughing when we turned around. 'Tex,' one of them said, 'let's start with you.'

"I glanced to the right and then to the left and then down at the only pair of cowboy boots in the room."

Lisa felt her eyebrows raise, but she couldn't take her eyes off Wyatt. He'd ended the tale with a self-mocking grimace and a shrug. The refrigerator chugged on, and a moth fluttered against the screen. Otherwise the room was quiet.

So, she thought, glimpsing the awkwardness in his expression, even pure-as-the-driven-snow sheriffs could be embarrassed and beaten up a little by life. She tried to see the humor in the situation, but the thought of him standing before her wearing nothing but his boots sent heat to places along her body she'd be better off not thinking about. Try as she might, she couldn't bring herself to laugh.

"Aren't you going to say anything?" he asked, stepping closer.

She shook her head.

He took another step as if he, too, felt the awareness arcing between them. "What would you say if I asked you to have dinner with me tomorrow night?"

Yes popped into her head. Right behind it came about a hundred things she'd promised to do. Sighing, she said, "I wasn't lying when I told Jason Tucker that I was going to be busy these next few weeks, Wyatt. I've decided to have a grand opening sale at the store. I thought I'd make up some fliers and pass them out at the Crazy Horse and in the diner. I might put a stack in the Clip & Curl and in

Ed's Barbershop, too. I'll have balloons for the kids, and cookies and lemonade for everybody. Today's already Thursday, and I couldn't be ready by this weekend. But I could have it a week from Saturday. What do you think?"

Wyatt thought he loved the way she talked, so full of life and excitement, but he loved the way she reached her hands to her head and winsomely removed the clip from her hair even more. Striding closer, he said, "I think it sounds like a great idea, but surely you'll have a little free time left for me."

She stopped suddenly and turned around. "I promised Jillian I'd help her plan her wedding. And you already know I'm working the supper crowd in Mel's Diner. DoraLee said she needs help, too."

"You're going to be working three jobs?"

She folded her arms and cast him an arch look. "It seems both DoraLee and Mel have had trouble finding good help. There's been a notable shortage of women in the area, you know."

Wyatt shook his head. Of course he knew. He'd been on the committee that had placed the ad in the papers. As far as he was concerned, that advertisement had been a success. It had brought Lisa to Jasper Gulch, hadn't it? He didn't especially appreciate the fact that all her time was going to be tied up, but he was a patient man. He could wait. At least a little while.

Holding her gaze, he took the few remaining steps separating them and reached for her hand. She sucked in a quick breath as if she didn't know what he was going to do. Hell, he didn't even know what he was going to do. Letting his instincts rule, he angled his head toward hers and began the slow descent to her mouth. Her eyelashes fluttered down once, but came up again, the expression in her eyes enough to make the blood surge through him stronger than ever.

He kissed her soundly, surely, thoroughly. By the time

he raised his face, his voice was little more than a husky rasp. "All right, Lisa, I can see you're going to be busy for the next week or so. But don't forget the barbecue Clayt's having for Luke and Jillian at the Carson Ranch the first Saturday in September. Everyone in town is invited, so there won't be any reason to keep the store open. You can go with me."

Lisa blinked, feeling strangely light-headed. Evidently Wyatt was having no such problem. He ambled to the door with a loose-jointed swagger that might as well have belonged to a cowboy. She followed him out to the porch and watched him put on his hat.

"See you later...Tex," she called to his back.

He turned around on the cracked sidewalk, and danged if he didn't smile. "Good night. Oh, and Lisa? You'd better carve a little time out of your busy schedule for me, because I can't be patient forever."

He continued on to his truck, started the engine and pulled away. Watching the taillights disappear around the corner, she slowly made her way back into the house. She yawned and stretched. And when she saw her reflection in a mirror across the room, she was smiling.

"You're smiling. I'm going to take that as a good sign," Jillian said, entering the front door of Lisa's shop.

Lisa blew her hair out of her eyes and faced her friend. By the time Jillian had closed the door, worry furrowed her brow. "I take that back. Your smile looks brittle. Does that mean the grand opening wasn't a success?"

Lisa closed the old-fashioned cash register and handed Wyatt his sack of purchases. Balloons had been bobbing merrily in front of the store since nine that morning, the breeze toying with the flyer she'd hung on the front door. Cookies filled a tray on a table in the center of the store, spare pitchers of lemonade cooling in an ice chest in the back room.

Glancing from Jillian to Wyatt and back again, Lisa said, "I don't know how you can say the grand opening sale wasn't successful, Jillian. After all, you bought a new jumper, DoraLee purchased a skirt, Mel a chambray shirt. Louetta came in at her usual time to browse, and a few of the bachelors stopped by. Even Wyatt, who claims he rates shopping up there with smashing his thumb in a car door, picked up two pairs of blue jeans and three T-shirts."

"That's it?" Jillian asked. "Nobody else came?"

Lisa shrugged. "Cletus bought a package of undershirts and a bolo tie to wear to your wedding. I guess I'll have better luck next time, huh?"

Wyatt strode around the store, pretending to look at the racks of women's casual wear, children's play clothes and men's blue jeans and shirts. Jillian was doing a darned good job of trying to cheer Lisa up, but he doubted Jillian was fooled by Lisa's feigned good cheer and good humor. One look at Lisa after the bell over the door jingled with Jillian's departure, and Wyatt wasn't fooled, either.

She was wearing an outfit off one of her own racks. It was made of some sort of gauzy, dark blue material that was cinched tightly at her waist. The skirt fluttered when she walked and stopped at the ankles of her black cowboy boots. At the start of the day, everything about her had been springy, from the curls in her hair all the way down to the bounce in her step. By noon the waves had all slid from her hair; by two the squareness had eased out of her shoulders, and sometime after three her steps had lost their bounce. Even the long fringe of her bangs couldn't hide the disappointment in her eyes or the dark smudges underneath them.

"Any word on my stolen car?" she asked.

Wyatt shook his head. "I followed up a few leads, but they didn't turn up anything substantial."

Tucking his package underneath his arm, he called, "Let's get out of here. There's a honky-tonk bar in Pierre that serves up juicy hamburgers, ice-cold beer, and boot-stomping music. What do you say we take in a little of all three?''

She sent him a smile that didn't quite make it to her eyes. "It sounds like fun, but I'm working for DoraLee tonight. Boomer finally convinced her that he isn't too young for her. They have a date."

Flattening a hand on either side of the cash register, Wyatt leaned closer. "You're filling in for DoraLee so she can go out with Boomer, which means that *I* can't take *you* out."

She looked up at him, the soul-deep expression in her brown eyes causing his heart to turn over in his chest. Damn, he couldn't even stay mad.

She hadn't been lying, more than a week ago, when she'd told him she was going to be extremely busy. True to her word, she'd put in long hours in her store, only to hurry next door to the diner or across the street to the Crazy Horse where she put in several more. She'd helped Jillian find the perfect wedding gown, and, with the wedding only three weeks away, plans for the upcoming event were running full speed ahead. In the midst of so many activities, Wyatt hadn't been able to take Lisa on a real date, but he'd gotten into the habit of driving her home. Twice he'd surprised her with pizza. A few days ago she'd whipped up a meal fit for a king. He hadn't known she could cook, but it wasn't her culinary skills that kept him coming back. It was her barely there smiles, the way she could tell a joke and turn a phrase, and the way she could turn his heart to mush with the barest brush of her lips across his.

Lisa leaned against her side of the counter. Moments ago she'd been ready to melt to the floor in a tired heap and bury her face in her hands. Staring into Wyatt's golden brown eyes, her heart thudded, and she began to think she might melt to the floor for an entirely different reason.

He leaned forward, and so did she, their faces drawing closer. Her lips parted, and her thoughts became hazy, her disappointment giving way to something as magical as a moonbeam and as pleasing as a sigh. His mouth touched hers, a sound echoing in the back of her throat, only to be answered in the back of his.

The door burst open and banged against the wall. She and Wyatt jerked apart. With her heart in her throat, she turned in time to see a child dart around a rack and scurry into a fitting room. Dropping her hand from her throat, Lisa glanced up at Wyatt, both their gazes going back to the curtain still fluttering on the other side of the store.

They were both across the room in seconds. Lisa dragged the curtain aside. A little girl with a spattering of freckles across her nose looked up at her as if she was a giant.

"Haley," Wyatt asked, "why are you hiding in this dressing room?"

The child's face brightened with recognition when she saw Wyatt, and she smiled, all peaches-and-cream innocence—until a boy's shoe fell from the bundle in her arms, landing on the floor with a heavy thud.

Chapter Six

"Haley," Wyatt repeated. "I asked you a question."

"I heard ya."

"And?"

"I'm thinking."

Wyatt crossed his arms and strummed his fingers on the sleeve of his shirt. When another shoe plopped to the floor, along with a pair of boy's underwear, Haley's eyes grew round and her smile slipped away. Creeping out of the dressing room like a puppy who'd just chewed his master's favorite shoe, she glanced around. Then made a mad dash for the door.

Wyatt beat her there.

He held the door shut with one hand and placed his other hand on her head. His voice rose in direct proportion to his dismay at discovering that her hair was damp. "Haley, have you been swimming?"

She wrinkled up her nose and squirmed from one foot to the other as if she was categorically running through a list of possible answers. Taking her narrow chin in his fingers, he angled her face up so he could see her eyes. "I want the truth, young lady."

"You do?"

Wyatt glanced at Lisa. Her eyes were large, but there was a smile lurking around the edges of her mouth. Turning his attention back to the ragamuffin in front of him, he said, "Yes, I do."

He'd always thought Haley Carson was a cute kid. Her hair was the same shade of brown her father's had been at that age. Although Victoria hadn't given her daughter much else, she had passed on her pretty brown eyes and beautiful skin. Haley would probably be a beauty some day—when she outgrew the scrapes on her knees and the dirt smudges on her clothes. When that happened, Clayt was going to be in even bigger trouble than he was now. He needed help with a capital *H*. If he wasn't so stubborn, he'd ask Mel to marry him and be done with it once and for all. But Clayt was stubborn. And so was Haley.

"Well?" Wyatt declared. "I'm waiting."

Heaving a huge sigh for someone so scrawny, Haley said, "I've been swimming."

"In Sugar Creek?"

"Yup."

"And whose clothes are those?"

"Jeremy Everts's."

"Why did you take Jeremy's clothes?"

"'Cuz he said I looked like a drowned rat."

"I see. That wasn't very nice of him, but it's no reason to steal his clothes. How would you like to have to walk home over a gravel road with bare feet, wearing nothing but a pair of swimming trunks?"

Wyatt didn't like the way Haley suddenly lowered her eyes to the toes of her canvas shoes. Swallowing his dread, he said, "Was—is—Jeremy wearing swimming trunks, young lady?"

The child's stony silence could only mean one thing.

Good Lord. Somewhere out there a little boy was roaming around, buck naked. Scrubbing a hand across his forehead, he said, "I think I'd better call your father."

"Do you hafta?"

Oh, yes, he definitely had to. Glancing at Lisa, he mouthed, "Keep an eye on her," then turned on his heels and strode to the phone.

Keeping the little girl in her line of vision, Lisa watched Wyatt walk away. Although he seemed in complete command of himself, there was a restless energy about him she hadn't noticed before. She had to admit, he definitely didn't look like a lawman who spent most of his time rescuing kittens out of trees.

Pulling her gaze from him wasn't easy. "Haley," she said, turning her attention back to the matter at hand. "Would you like a cookie and a glass of lemonade?"

The child turned up her nose at the lemonade, but accepted two chocolate-chip cookies. Munching, she meandered around a rack of women's jumpers, coming to a stop in front of the shelves of lingerie. She stroked her hand over a pair of black panties and a matching push-up bra. Chewing loudly, she said, "I wish I could wear pretty underwear like this."

Lisa held the item up for the child to see. "I'm afraid this won't fit you for another few years."

"I know. My boobies have to grow first. Do you think they'll grow as big as yours?"

Lisa swallowed a gasp. It took a lot to surprise her. Haley Carson had done it without batting an eye. Finding her voice, Lisa said, "They're called breasts, but Haley? The size doesn't matter. I have a feeling you're going to be beautiful no matter what size bra you wear."

"Really?"

In that instant, Haley reminded her of Melody. Why were women so insecure about their bodies? Mel thought her breasts were too small, Lisa had always worried that hers were the only thing men noticed, and Haley couldn't wait to get some, period.

Her friend, Corinna, would have known exactly what to say to a nine-year-old girl who'd just admitted that she'd gone skinny-dipping with a boy and wished she was old enough to wear pretty underclothes. Unfortunately Cori was in Madison, which meant that Lisa was all this little girl had. Taking a deep breath for courage, she said, "You know, Haley, it's not a good idea to let boys see you na-ked. Not unless you and he are married. Are you married, Haley?"

Haley raised her big brown eyes to Lisa's. "No, silly. But I made him turn around while I got in."

"Oh, well, that's good." Curious, Lisa lowered her voice to a conspiratorial whisper and said, "What about when Jeremy got in the water?"

"He made me cover my eyes."

"I see."

"But I peeked."

Lisa did everything in her power to keep the surprise and the grin off her face, but it wasn't easy. Haley Carson was something else. No wonder Wyatt and Cletus had both shaken their heads and declared that Clayt needed help raising his little girl.

"Lisa? If you think I'm pretty, why did Jeremy say I look like a drowned rat?"

"Well," Lisa answered, "sometimes boys say things like that when they like a girl."

"Why?"

Lisa shrugged, thinking that now probably wasn't a good time to tell Haley that she'd probably spend the rest of her life trying to understand why men do the things they do.

"Has Uncle Wyatt ever said that to you?"

Lisa's gaze automatically trailed to the front of the store where Wyatt was talking in hushed tones over the phone.

"By the time boys grow up, they usually find other ways to get a girl's attention."

"Has Uncle Wyatt gotten your attention?"

"Once or twice."

"Does he like you?"

Haley's innocent question thrummed a slow, dreamy chord deep inside Lisa. "Yes, I think he does."

"Do you like him?"

A month ago she would have denied the possibility. A week ago she would have denied the feelings of elation and buoyancy such a question sent to her chest. Today she looked Haley straight in the eyes and said, "Yes, I like him very much."

Haley tugged on Lisa's sleeve and whispered, "I like Uncle Wyatt, too. Do you *hafta* tell him?"

"That I like him?"

"No."

Lisa stared down into the little girl's round brown eyes, trying to understand what it was the child was asking. "That you went swimming without your bathing suit? He already knows, sweetheart."

"I know that. Do we have to tell him I peeked?"

Smiling warmly, Lisa cast a glance at Wyatt, who was still talking on the telephone. "I'll keep that a secret. On one condition."

The child's eyes narrowed suspiciously. "What condition?"

Leaning down, Lisa whispered in Haley's ear. "I won't tell Wyatt you peeked. *If* you promise that you won't go skinny-dipping with a boy again."

Haley skewed her mouth to one side, obviously giving the *condition* a great deal of thought. As if she realized it was the best deal she could make under the circumstances, she nodded and placed her small hand in Lisa's for a formal handshake.

Wyatt glanced over his shoulder, wondering why Lisa

and Haley were shaking hands as if they were sealing a new foreign policy. That little kid was going to be the death of Clayt yet. Last month she'd stolen food off Lisa and Jillian's porch. This month it was skinny-dipping in Sugar Creek. He shuddered to think what she would do next.

He knew she missed her mother, but he sure as hell didn't know why. As far as he was concerned, Victoria had never been much of a mother. Haley had a lot going for her. She was extremely bright, and when she was cleaned up a little, she really was a cute kid. Her bangs must have dried while she was running, because they were sticking straight up. Her pigtails were askew, her shirt was dirty, her shorts grass stained. She definitely needed a feminine touch. Maybe Haley didn't miss her mother as much as she missed having a woman in her life. Wyatt wished to high heaven Clayt would wake up and give Mel a chance. After all, his sister had been in love with Clayt Carson since the third grade. And if anyone could handle Haley, Melody could.

From what he'd gleaned so far, Clayt had been under the impression that his darling daughter was at the library with her new friend, Jeremy Everts. Wyatt hadn't enjoyed setting Clayt straight, but there were some things better said in person.

Lowering his voice a little more, he said, "No, everything's all right. Haley's here with me.... No, she's fine. But I think I'd rather not get into this over the phone. Haley and I will be there as soon as I return little Jeremy Everts's clothes.... Yes, that's what I said.... No, you don't have to get up a search party for the boy. I think I know exactly where he is.... I already told you. She's fine.... Okay, I'll see you soon."

He replaced the telephone and turned around, surprised to find Lisa and Haley waiting for him a few feet away. "You can take me to my father now," Haley said, tucking her hand into his as if she were a human sacrifice waiting to be led to the mouth of an active volcano.

Wyatt squeezed the small hand in his and glanced at Lisa, hoping her expression would give him a clue as to what had just taken place between her and Haley. She looked back at him and winked as if she had the situation under control. Her smile lighted up her face, but it didn't hide the dark smudges beneath her eyes.

"You're really something, you know that?" he said, that age-old heat pulsing through him all over again.

"Yeah, sure. I'm really something. Now go on. Go do whatever it is a good sheriff is supposed to do in a situation like this. Oh, and, Wyatt? Take good care of Haley. She reminds me a lot of me at that age."

Lisa wasn't surprised by Wyatt's sharply drawn breath, but somebody could have knocked her over with a feather when Haley shook her hand free of his and hurtled herself straight at Lisa's midsection. The arms encircling her waist were strong for someone so thin, and left Lisa feeling weak in the knees.

The hug only lasted a matter of seconds, but the warmth it had sent straight to her heart stayed with her long after Wyatt left, Haley's fingers held firmly in one hand, Jeremy Everts's clothes clutched tight in the other. Alone in her store, Lisa went about her chores. She packed up the cookies she'd baked at two this morning and dumped the lemonade down the drain. After locking the front door, she straightened a few stacks of blue jeans that had gotten messed earlier. Tucking a pitcher beneath each arm, she ducked into the alley via the back door and slipped into the diner the same way.

Pies were cooling on the counter in the diner's old kitchen. Lunch dishes were stacked, shiny and clean, next to the sink. As usual the place looked neat and tidy, but Mel was nowhere in sight.

Since it was a little early for the supper crowd, Lisa

assumed her friend had gone up to her apartment for a few minutes. She ran soapy water into the deep steel sink. Watching the bubbles form, she spread her hand wide over the exact place Haley Carson had pressed her cheek and went weak in the knees all over again.

Haley Carson was amazing. Even more amazing was the fact that the child *liked* her. She hadn't expected to appeal to children. Oh, she loved Cori's daughter, Allison, to pieces, but Allison was sixteen, now, and had known Lisa most of her young life. Haley was nine and had only just met Lisa. The girl was a holy terror, right down to her freckles and skinned knees, but she was smart as a whip. And she liked Lisa. Imagine that. A little kid who hadn't known her forever liked her.

Her dreams might yet come true. She'd expected things to fall into place in the normal sequence. First her store would be a success. Then she'd fall in love, marry, make a home and eventually make babies.

When had her life ever followed a normal sequence?

It didn't matter. Haley liked her. Someday Lisa's own sons or daughters would *love* her, and so would her future children's father. She felt drunk on the possibilities, on airy hopes that would someday become reality.

Lisa washed the pitchers she'd borrowed from Mel, humming all the while, practically bursting with renewed anticipation. Things were going to work out just fine. Why had she ever questioned it? So her grand opening sale hadn't been a huge success. Tomorrow was another day, right?

Voices carried from the dining room. Turning, Lisa had a smile all ready for Mel. She made it as far as the swinging kitchen door before she realized that neither of the voices belonged to her friend.

"I just ran into Mel at the Clip & Curl. Said she'd be right along, and that we should make ourselves comfortable in our usual seats."

Lisa stopped, one hand on the door. Not wanting to eavesdrop, she strode back to the counter and tried not to listen.

"I asked my sister, Thelma, to do a little checking for me. You remember Thelma, don't you, Opal?"

"Yes, of course, Isabell."

"She used to be a clerk in the sheriff's office over in Aberdeen, so I asked her to punch Lisa Markman's name into the computer and see what she came up with. And it's just as I suspected. That little harlot has quite a past, let me tell you."

"Now, Isabell. You don't know for certain she's a harlot."

"With that walk and that body! What else could she be? I knew it the first time she interrupted the town meeting last month to pass out her fliers. A woman like her with scandal in her past can only bring scandal to our peaceful town."

"My, yes, yes, I do believe that's true."

Lisa pressed her hands to the counter's cool surface, her smile slowly draining from her face. She didn't want to hear any more, but she couldn't seem to find the strength to raise her hands to her ears.

"Opal, you'd think Wyatt McCully would know better than to get hooked up with that little hussy. Thelma said her father once went to prison, and that's just the beginning. You know what they say. The acorn doesn't fall far from the tree. I'm not surprised *she* hasn't realized that the fine women of the Ladies Aid Society are boycotting her store, but I never would have believed that our kindhearted Wyatt McCully would get mixed up with the likes of her."

Hurt squeezed like a fist around Lisa's heart. She closed her eyes and gave herself a mental shake. That's what you get for eavesdropping, Markman.

In reality, she hadn't been eavesdropping. Opal Graham

and Isabell Pruitt had whispers that could penetrate solid brick.

She had to get out of there. Leaving the pitchers to drip-dry in the drainer, she took a deep breath and slipped out the back door.

The air in the alley was stifling hot, the late-August sun even hotter here where the buildings blocked the wind. She hurried inside her store, then stood leaning against the back door until her eyes adjusted to the dim interior.

She had to pull herself together. A long time ago she'd grown accustomed to bigots and snobs who sat in self-righteous judgment of others. She'd known Isabell and Opal didn't approve of her, but she'd been so caught up in her growing feelings for Wyatt she hadn't realized that there was a bigger reason than a poor economy that the only person to enter her store on a regular basis, other than her friends, was Louetta Graham.

The acorn doesn't fall far from the tree, hmm? Well, in Louetta's case, the acorn had somehow turned into a willow tree. Although Lisa was glad that Louetta hadn't taken after her mother, it didn't remove the sting from Opal's and Isabell's words.

She looked around her quiet store, at the fruits of her labors, at the racks of clothes she'd painstakingly arranged. Most of the items remained exactly where she'd put them. Now she knew why.

She hadn't opened this store to get rich. She wanted to provide an honest service for honest people and earn an honest living at the same time. More than anything, she wanted to fit in. Why had that always been so difficult to do?

She sank to the floor slowly, her back against the door, her elbows resting on her knees, her head bowed. She must have sat there contemplating that question for a long time, because when she came out of her trance, she was appalled to see that it was nearly seven o'clock. She was due at the Crazy Horse in minutes.

Deciding the nervous breakdown she deserved would have to wait, she climbed to her feet, turned out the lights and let herself out her store's front door.

"Hey, Lisa. We could use another round of beers back here."

If it had been up to her, she would have served the rowdy bachelors mugs of strong coffee. But DoraLee said a man's hangover was his own concern, so Lisa took five long-necked bottles from the cooler and placed them on a tray.

She put a bottle by each man's elbow and gave them all a wink they'd come to expect. If anybody noticed that her smiles seemed a little forced tonight, they didn't mention it to her.

"Did your daddy really go to prison?" Ben Jacobs asked, his voice carrying from one end of the bar to the other.

"Yeah, Ben, he really did," she answered.

"What did he do, rob a bank?" the man sitting next to Ben asked.

She tucked the tray beneath her arm and said, "Give that man a cigar."

The bachelors chortled, and although Lisa had accompanied her rejoinder with a semblance of a smile, she didn't think it was funny. She never had.

She'd been in Jasper Gulch long enough to know that word traveled fast out here, gossip even faster. While serving up beers and pretzels, she'd heard several references to Haley Carson's escapades, but the bachelors seemed more interested in *her* past.

"So you ran away from home when you were fifteen?"

"A few weeks before, actually."

"You once lived in a deserted warehouse?"

"Mmm-hmm."

"That's a mighty dangerous world out there for a young girl. How'd ya eat?"

"Oh, I managed."

"You must have come into contact with some mighty rough characters."

"Not as many as you might think."

"Ever meet any real-live pimps?"

"One or two."

Every question was more difficult to answer, every drink more difficult to serve. DoraLee bustled in shortly after eleven, the scent of her perfume arriving a full minute before she did. She was wearing a low-cut blouse, blue eye shadow and ruby red lipstick. Lisa had never been so relieved to see a friendly face in her life.

"Hey, Lisa, are the streets really crawling with crack addicts?" Karl Hanson called.

DoraLee narrowed her eyes and placed one hand on her ample hip. "You boys watch too much television. Don't you have anything better to do than ask stupid questions? If you want Lisa to stay, you'd better be on your best behavior from now on."

There was a flurry of shuffling feet and murmured apologies. After that, the talk turned to more normal topics such as the price of beef, the next roundup, and the continued shortage of women out here.

DoraLee bustled around the bar, talking a mile a minute. Before Lisa knew how it had happened, she was sitting on one of the bar stools staring at a shot of tequila, a slice of lemon and a salt shaker.

"There, there, sugar, you look like you could use a stiff drink."

After a long pause, during which Lisa fought for self-control, she sighed and pushed the shot glass away. "I don't think getting drunk is going to help, DoraLee."

"Getting drunk never does, but a shot of tequila might put a little color in your cheeks."

Lisa eyed the sole proprietor of the Crazy Horse Saloon, thinking how nice it was to be on the receiving end of that warm smile. "Then you heard about the boycott."

DoraLee made a most unbecoming sound. "I wouldn't mind five minutes alone with Isabell Pruitt. Oh, she's never had anything to do with me, and truthfully, I never much cared. But what she's doing to your store is horrible. Why, the old biddy wouldn't know a good person if one bit her on her bony butt."

Lisa smiled for real for the first time in hours. "How was your date with Boomer?"

DoraLee's hand fluttered to her coiffed blond hair, and an honest-to-goodness blush crept to her cheeks. "Oh, it was fine, real fine. But you look done in, sugar. If you don't want the drink, at least let me get one of the boys to give you a ride home."

Giving DoraLee a tired smile, Lisa slid to her feet. "Thanks, DoraLee, but the walk will probably do me good. I'll talk to you tomorrow, okay?"

Someone called to DoraLee for another drink, and Lisa ducked into the back room, then slowly trudged home.

Wyatt pulled to a stop in front of Lisa's house and promptly cut the engine. It was one o'clock in the morning. He'd just come from the Crazy Horse. Before that, he'd been in Murdo where he'd been summoned to settle a barroom dispute. It had taken a while to get to the bottom of the problem. After listening to a dozen versions of the brawl, he'd finally arrested two local ranchers, who were sleeping it off in the low-security cells in the back room in the sheriff's office right now. Before that, he'd spent an hour at Clayt's place, talking about Haley.

The full moon might have accounted for all the strange behavior that had taken place tonight, but it wasn't the moon he was looking at as he strode up Lisa's sidewalk. Every light in the house was on. He didn't know whether that was a good sign or not. Taking the porch steps two at a time, he gave the screen door a yank. And stopped cold. The door was locked.

He raised his fist and knocked. Within seconds Lisa appeared. She looked right at him, then deftly lifted the hook, turning around again without saying a word.

Wyatt opened the door and followed, tossing his hat to the back of an old wooden rocking chair on his way by. He found Lisa sitting at the kitchen table, ledgers and receipts and forms spread around her.

"You know," he said, taking a chair opposite her, "I've had warmer welcomes from people I've pulled over for speeding."

She raised her eyes from a receipt and stared right at him, but she didn't smile. He didn't quite know what to make of the cool, composed look in her eyes or of the level tone in her voice when she said, "I suppose you've heard."

"I ran into my grandfather at the Crazy Horse."

There was an instant's squeezing hurt in her eyes. She blinked, and it was gone.

She jumped up and spun around, all in one motion, her dress fluttering in her wake. He'd glimpsed a restless energy about her before, but tonight it was ten times more pronounced. She strode to the refrigerator, only to flounce to the opposite wall, sputtering about small-minded people all the while.

Wyatt nodded when he thought she expected him to, and generally let her rant. He'd been prepared to find her eyes swollen from crying. He wouldn't have even been surprised if she'd been a little bit tipsy. But he hadn't expected her to be angry. Staring at her profile, at her delicate nose and the haughty angle of her chin, he felt something flicker deep inside, and pride slowly filled him to the point of bursting.

He rose, too, but more slowly, surely, purposefully. Lisa was so busy flouncing from one end of the room to the other she didn't seem to notice. He caught the clean scent of soap and shampoo on one of her trips by. Her feet were bare, and her hair looked shiny in some places, damp in others. He didn't know where she got her dress, but he doubted it had come from one of the racks in her own store. It was long, almost ankle length, and was covered in flowers the colors of dusk—muted grays, shady blues and faint traces of lavender. It looked so soft you could almost hear it whisper every time she moved. The neckline scooped low in front, the material following the contours of her lush body as if it had been made for her alone. He could see the smooth slope of her breasts, bare except for that soft fabric, so beautiful he ached.

"All these weeks I've been working in my store, arranging displays, lowering prices, looking for bargains, thinking it was just a matter of time before people started coming in. Stupid, huh? Now that I've had time to think about it, I'm not really surprised that Isabell Pruitt has judged me and found me unfit. After all, there are bigots everywhere, right? What hurts even more are the bachelors' reaction."

Wyatt leaned in the doorway, within hearing range, but out of the way of her pacing. "What about the bachelors, Lisa?"

She stopped long enough to look at him. For a moment he thought she might ask him to leave. But she twirled around again and said, "Since I've moved to Jasper Gulch, I've gone out with a dozen of the Jasper Gents. They were all nice enough, but they all spent the majority of the evening talking about themselves. Not one of them thought to ask about me. Until tonight, that is. Now, everybody wants to know about my past. Why wouldn't they? It's the stuff talk shows are made of, isn't it?

"'What was it like living on the street?' they asked. 'How did you eat?' The question behind that one is, 'What did you have to sell to eat?'

"I may have stolen to eat, but I never sold myself. Just once I wish somebody would be interested in *me*, what I am inside, who I am inside. What's my favorite color, my favorite food, my favorite song?"

"Lisa?" he asked quietly.

"But that isn't as interesting as sordid details, is it? Oh, no, they want to know if I ever met a real-live pimp, and a real-live..."

"Leese."

Lisa stopped pacing and slowly turned around. Wyatt was leaning in the doorway on the other side of the room. His eyes looked dark and unfathomable from here, his lips set in a straight line. "What's your favorite color?"

Tears blurred her vision, thickened her throat. She wasn't sure if it was because of the way Wyatt looked at that moment, all long and lean and golden, or the way he'd whispered her name.

"No one has ever called me that."

He straightened without taking his eyes from hers. "Someone does now."

Tension drained out of her, her agitation evaporated, and her thoughts slowed, until everything inside her was as still as the night. Her heart beat a gentle rhythm, and one tear trailed down her cheek.

It was so easy to get lost in the way he looked at her. When he gestured to the living room and told her she must be exhausted after putting in a long day at the store and then a long night at the Crazy Horse, she followed his advice and walked into the next room and settled herself in the deep cushions of her own sofa.

He sat next to her, close, but not quite touching, the dim

bulb in the lamp next to the couch the only light in the room. He talked about the brawl he'd broken up in Murdo, and how he'd found Jeremy Everts hiding behind a shelter belt of trees near the creek, as naked as the day he was born. He described the expression on Clayt's face when he'd learned that Haley had been skinny-dipping, his voice working over her in waves, lulling her, calming her, soothing her.

"Do you mind if I help myself to a beer, Lisa?" he asked.

"Mmm," she answered.

Wyatt rose from the couch carefully and strode into the kitchen as quietly as possible. A peek inside her refrigerator confirmed his suspicions. There was fruit and vegetables and milk and juice and left-over pasta and a half-empty bottle of champagne that didn't have any bubbles. But there wasn't any beer.

Being careful to walk around the major creaks in the floor, he went back to the living room where a threadbare carpet muffled his footsteps. Lisa had turned her head so that her cheek was resting along the back cushion. Her eyes were closed, her breathing even. She didn't move when he leaned over her. Exhaustion had finally caught up with her; she was sound asleep.

She didn't wake when he grasped her upper arms and gently laid her down. Her breasts felt so soft and warm where they brushed the backs of his hands. His mouth went dry, the blood pounding in his ears. He didn't move, barely breathed, his hormones on a rampage, his body drawing taut.

Finally managing to pull his gaze away, he ran a hand through his hair and gave himself a mental kick for ogling a sleeping woman. He lifted her feet next and carefully covered her with a soft throw that had been draped over the back of the couch. She sighed in her sleep and snuggled into its warmth. Her hair fell across her cheek, a dark swath against her golden skin. Her eyelashes cast shadows on her cheeks, her lips neither smiling nor frowning.

Ignoring the strange aching in his limbs, he turned off the light. Using the illumination of the porch light shining through the window, he slowly made his way to her front door.

Lisa turned her head and tried to roll over, but was stopped by some sort of immovable object. Where in the world was she? Fighting her way up from a dark, drugging sleep, she took a deep breath. Someone had fried bacon. It couldn't have been Jillian. She couldn't boil water.

Lisa opened her eyes and came face-to-face with the back of her sofa. She didn't remember falling asleep down here. She didn't remember falling asleep, period. She remembered ranting and raving in her kitchen and then relaxing to the soothing cadence of Wyatt's voice.

Wyatt.

She bolted upright and quickly found her feet. Pushing her hair out of her eyes, she padded into the kitchen. Wyatt was sitting at her table, a newspaper spread out in front of him, a mug of coffee and a plate of bacon off to one side. He looked up when she entered and calmly lifted the mug to his lips.

"Have you been here all night?" she asked.

The newspaper crinkled as he turned the page, his mug making a clunking noise as he placed it on the table. Reaching for a slice of bacon, he said, "I spent most of the night on a cot in my office keeping watch over my two 'drunk and disorderlies.' Their wives arrived to take them home about an hour ago. Honestly, there isn't much the court system could do to top the punishment those two women are going to inflict upon their men."

Lisa found herself nodding in agreement, and she had no idea why. "Where's Jillian?"

"She left a little while ago. She and Luke are going to paint his kitchen today. He's thrilled."

Still groggy, it took a moment for Lisa to absorb the fact that she'd been completely oblivious to Wyatt's departure last night, not to mention Jillian's return home from her date and her departure again this morning. Pouring herself a mug of coffee, she said, "I must have been out like a light."

"You look much more rested this morning, and very pretty."

Lisa turned around slowly, the coffee never making it to her lips. She knew exactly how she looked. She'd slept in her clothes, for heaven's sake. Her hair was mussed, her dress wrinkled. Staring into Wyatt's warm brown eyes, she'd never felt more beautiful.

Recovering her voice and her equilibrium, she said, "Would you like some eggs to go with that bacon, Wyatt?"

He folded his newspaper and unfolded his legs, slowly rising to his feet. "I can't stay. I have a report to file and a visit to pay to the owner of the bar that got wrecked during last night's brawl."

"I see," she said, although she didn't really. If he had to leave again, why had he come over this morning?

As if reading her mind, he said, "I asked you a question last night, and you never answered."

"I'm afraid last night is a little fuzzy. What did you ask me?"

Church bells chimed in the distance as he came closer, his gaze unwavering. "What's your favorite color?"

Lisa's vision became hazy, her thoughts dreamy, her body warm. In fact, she was pretty sure the hand pressed to the counter at her back was all that was keeping her from sliding to the floor. "Blue," she whispered. "My favorite color is the lightest, palest shade of blue."

She didn't have the presence of mind to ask him why

he wanted to know. When his lips touched hers, she didn't care. She wound her arms around his back and kissed him, a budding joy spreading through her.

He lifted his head and dragged in a ragged breath of air. Feeling warm and wanted, she ran her finger along the straight line of his jaw as he said, "If I didn't have to drive down to Murdo, I wouldn't. I'd stay and..."

His voice trailed away, straight to her senses. "I know, Wyatt. We both have a lot to do, but I'm not going anywhere. Tomorrow's another day, isn't it?"

Wyatt stared at her, absorbing the implications of what she'd just said. She was letting him know, in so many words, that she wasn't giving up, not on her store, not on the town, not on him. The woman had more spunk than anyone he knew. But she was right. Tomorrow was another day, and he could hardly wait to see what it would bring.

"You're right, Leese. We have all the time in the world."

He left within minutes, taking the smile she gave him with him when he went.

Chapter Seven

"What's she doin'?"

"I don't know. I cain't see that far anymore."

"Hey, Cletus, it looks like she's plantin' flowers."

Wyatt slowed his steps and glanced around, coming to a complete stop in front of his office. It wasn't unusual to see his grandfather shooting the breeze with one of his old cronies on his favorite bench in front of the post office. But the sight of Lisa planting flowers in an old barrel next to her store wasn't a normal Monday morning occurrence.

Folks up and down Main Street were standing around talking behind their hands. The usual old-timers were sitting on stools underneath the faded awning over Ed's Barbershop across the street. A couple of young boys were drinking sodas by the gas pump at Bart's Gas Station on the corner. And Edith Fergusson, the town's oldest history teacher, was standing with Bonnie Trumble in front of the Clip & Curl, wearing pink curlers and a matching plastic cape, whispering to beat the band.

"She's really plantin' flowers?" Cletus asked.

"Yep," Roy Everts said, scratching his craggy chin.

"Why would she plant flowers at the end of August? I s'pose she could be plantin' mums," he said, answering his own question.

Wyatt pulled at the brim of his hat, a grin stealing across his face. His eyesight was twenty-twenty, and those weren't mums Lisa was planting.

"Wait," Roy declared, "it looks more like bright pink petunias to me. That doesn't seem like somethin' a person who's ashamed of herself would do, does it?"

"Nope," Cletus answered. "It don't seem like somethin' a person who's gonna let a few narrow-minded biddies run her out of town would do, either. She's a spitfire, that's for sure."

Wyatt had never felt so much pride fill his chest. Cletus was right. Lisa wasn't running away. She was making a statement. She wasn't denying her past, nor was she ashamed of it. She was putting down roots, literally and figuratively. Despite the fact that someone had stolen her car, and folks had boycotted her store, she was going to stay. In the process, she was coloring their drab town in her own unique way.

She chose that moment to look his way, her gaze meeting his from halfway down the block. She smiled, and the pride in his chest moved over to make room for the heat that pulsed with a life of its own. He lifted his hand and did his best to smile in return, but it wasn't easy when what he wanted to do was march down the street and kiss her in front of every wagging tongue in the county.

"That woman ought to give lessons," Mel said, sliding to a stop next to her brother.

Wyatt nodded without tearing his gaze away from Lisa.

"You don't need to take lessons from anybody," Cletus said. "You're a fine-lookin' young woman with a strong back, to boot."

"Gee, Granddad," Melody muttered, scuffing the toe of her shoe in the loose dirt that had gathered in one of the cracks of the sidewalk. "Such flowery praise is liable to go to my head."

"Not a chance. You're too sensible for that."

Even if Wyatt hadn't seen Mel cringe, he couldn't have missed the succinct cussword she muttered under her breath.

"There's no need to swear, young lady," Cletus insisted. "You just lay low for a little while longer. The time ain't quite right for you yet. Last month I got Luke and Jillian together. This month I'm workin' on Wyatt and Lisa. I'll get to you as soon as possible, don'choo worry."

"You gonna take credit for the end of the drought, too, old man?" Roy grumbled.

"Of course not. That was God's doin', but He works in some mighty mysterious ways, and so does love. You wait and see."

Wyatt glanced at the advertisement luring women to Jasper Gulch that was hanging in the window in the post office and had to agree with his grandfather. Oh, he didn't think Cletus deserved all the credit for bringing Lisa to town. After all, it had been the town council's idea to put the ad in the paper in the first place. But Wyatt believed in giving credit where credit was due. He'd thank his grandfather, the town council, even his lucky stars, because the truth was, he'd never known another woman like Lisa Markman, and he was infinitely glad she'd come to Jasper Gulch.

"Is Lisa scheduled to work at the diner tonight?" he asked his sister.

Mel nodded, and Wyatt almost echoed her earlier exclamation. It was getting downright frustrating. When he wasn't competing with the local bachelors for Lisa's attention, he was competing with her various jobs for her time.

He ran his hand over his chin, deep in thought. Mel wasn't the only McCully who had a lot of backbone. She wasn't the only McCully whose patience was wearing thin, either. He didn't know how much chance his sister had of turning Clayt Carson's head, but Wyatt knew for a fact that Lisa hadn't accepted a date with any of the bachelors in weeks, and she accepted a ride home with *him* every day. He should have known she wasn't the kind of woman who would curl up and play dead. Actually, he wouldn't have been surprised if she'd stuck her tongue out at those old biddies who were boycotting her store. He was beginning to realize that Lisa had far too much class for that.

She rose to her feet in one fluid motion, swiped at the dirt on her knees and hands, then glanced to the side and looked right at him. Wyatt didn't know what was going through her mind, but he knew what was going through his body. He just didn't know how much longer he could stand the torture of wanting and not having, of needing and not claiming.

Giving him her notorious wink, she gathered up her spade and empty flower containers and walked into her store. He turned on his heels and headed for his own office where he managed to tamp down the need flaring through him, but not the intensity.

Could Lisa really see herself as a lesser person because of things that had happened in her past that had been out of her control? Wyatt had done his best to be patient while she came to the realization that she was good enough for any man she chose. It was about time someone pointed it out to her. It just so happened he knew the perfect man for the job.

"Need a lift?"

Lisa smiled to herself, the look over her shoulder automatic and completely unnecessary. She would have recognized the low, smooth timbre in Wyatt's voice anywhere. With a sassy lift of her eyebrows, she said, "That depends. Are you going my way?"

"I am now."

She didn't know how Wyatt did it, but he showed up just as she was getting off work every night, whether from the diner or the Crazy Horse. He always asked her—in that gentlemanly way he had—if she needed a lift, and she always answered with a flirty question of her own.

Seconds later she was sitting in the passenger seat of Wyatt's pickup, the wind fluttering through her hair as she exchanged idle chatter with a man who made her wits feel anything but idle.

"Where are we going?" she asked, glancing at the unfamiliar surroundings.

"I'm taking you home."

"I hate to be the one to point this out," she said over the country-western song playing on the radio, "but this isn't the way to my house."

"That's because I'm not taking you to your house. I'm taking you to mine."

Before she could respond one way or another, he pulled into a gravel driveway and brought his truck to a stop. "It's not much," he said, "but it's home."

Lisa peered into the dusky twilight, taking in the house in one sweeping glance. The two-story clapboard structure with its steep tin roof and small front porch wasn't much different from any other house in Jasper Gulch. But this was where Wyatt lived, and she was curious to see more.

He led the way to a back door and let them in without turning a key. The kitchen had a sixties feel to it, which was probably when it had been upgraded. There was rooster wallpaper on the walls and threadbare curtains, billowing over windows opened wide to accommodate the cooling breezes that never stopped blowing in from the plains.

Wyatt turned on the light, and Lisa strode directly to his refrigerator. "Do you mind?" she asked.

He shrugged. "Be my guest."

She opened the refrigerator door and peered inside, explaining, "Ivy always says you can tell a lot about a man by looking in his refrigerator. And it's just as I suspected. You eat most of your meals at the diner."

"What do you make of that?"

She had a rejoinder all ready, but the sound of crinkling paper drew her around, and the words never made it to her lips. Wyatt was standing a few feet away, one hand on his hip, the other hand holding out a package wrapped in pale blue tissue paper.

"What's that?" she asked inanely.

"A present."

"I figured that much out for myself. Who's it for?"

"It's for you."

Lisa couldn't remember the last time a man had bought her a gift. She couldn't remember the last time she'd felt so ill equipped to accept one. Although she'd tried not to let on, the past few days had taken a toll on her. She'd answered countless questions about her past from the Jasper Gents, and had dodged several of their advances. Wyatt was different. He didn't ask about her childhood, and he didn't make unwanted advances. He was a gentleman in every sense of the word.

Now he was standing a few feet away in his own kitchen, wearing faded jeans and one of the T-shirts he'd bought at her grand opening sale, making no attempt to hide the fact that he was watching her every move. His eyes took on a masculine haziness, his voice dipping low as he said, "I'm dying to see what you make of this."

She swallowed and reached for the package. She could tell from its weight and feel that it was some sort of clothing. Suddenly she remembered the last time she'd been given a gift by a man. It had been tight, backless and red.

Carrying the package to the table, she took a deep breath, ran a finger underneath a piece of tape, then deftly lifted the paper.

"Do you like it?"

Wyatt's question drew her gaze. One look at his face and she couldn't look away. His hair had been cut recently, the overhead lights streaking the dark blond tresses with gold. His face held quiet dignity, and was shaped by strong angles and masculine hollows that would never go out of style.

Gesturing to the gift in her hand, he said, "I thought you might want to wear it to Luke and Jillian's engagement barbecue this weekend. What do you think?"

"I think it's lovely."

As one second followed another, his expression changed in the subtlest of ways. "I did a little shopping in Pierre this afternoon. I had no idea what I was looking for, but when I saw this, it made me think of you."

Lisa could think of nothing to say. The dress was beautiful, virginal almost. It was made of a soft, knit fabric in the palest shade of blue she'd ever seen. It had long sleeves, a softly gathered skirt and a rounded neckline, and was no doubt the kind of dress that made a woman feel beautiful and cherished and wanted.

His boots creaked slightly as he took a step closer. "They say it takes twelve acts of kindness to make up for one negative deed. And you haven't let the Isabell Pruitts and Opal Grahams in this town drive you away. You're quite a woman, Lisa Markman."

Lisa had never been prone to tears, but they filled her eyes and thickened her throat for the second time in a matter of days. Wyatt thought she was quite a woman. She'd never thought of herself that way. She hadn't thought one simple gift could cause so many feelings to settle in her chest, either. She felt warmed by his smile, flushed with heat from the way he was looking at her, and so full of airy hopes and dreams it took her breath away.

"Oh, Wyatt."

"Why don't you come here and say that?"

With a slow, secret smile, she sashayed closer, marveling at the fact that a man who claimed he rated shopping right up there with smashing his thumb in a car door had taken the time to *shop* for her. Breathing in the scent of freshly showered man and late-summer breezes, she placed her hand on his shoulder. With a slow lift of her chin, she looked into his eyes and asked, "Now what was it you wanted me to say?"

Wyatt's entire body tightened, starting with his throat, moving down to his chest, steadily working its way lower. He'd dated a handful of women over the years. He'd even thought he was in love once, but he'd never met a woman who could ignite his desire and rouse his passion with one arch of her eyebrows, one haughty lift of her chin or one innocent little phrase issued with so much provocation it sent desire shooting through him.

"Wyatt?"

"Hmm?" His response came out as a deep rasp and said more about the need building inside him than any word could have.

"What are you doing?" she whispered.

Lowering his face an inch at a time, he said, "I'm savoring the sight and smell of you. I'm prolonging the moment, and it's taking every ounce of willpower I possess."

His voice was like corduroy, smooth as velvet if you went with the grain, course if you brushed against it. Everything inside Lisa responded to the sound, making her skin feel warm, her thoughts dreamy.

As his face came closer, her vision blurred, her lips parted and her breath caught in her throat. Gazing up at him, she whispered, "What would happen if you let go of your self-control?"

He pulled her to him so fast and so hard the air whooshed out of her lungs. His lips found hers in the middle of her next breath, her arms winding around his waist, her hands skimming along the muscles in his strong back, her fingers massaging, seeking, finding.

His kiss was urgent, rousing, delicious. His hands were working their own brand of magic on her, pliantly molding her tighter to his body, gliding to her waist and slowly inching lower. Lisa's head tipped back, her mouth opening beneath his. Still the kiss went on. And on. Every touch of their hands somehow intensified the joining of their lips, their breath and their sighs.

When his hand found its way between their bodies, his fingers spreading wide over her breast, kneading her flesh with a unique mixture of reverence and hot-blooded desire, she groaned his name. Her back arched, and she closed her eyes, her thoughts fragmenting.

"So beautiful," he whispered. "And so perfect."

His voice was nothing more than a husky rasp now, stroking across her senses in a way she never wanted to end. Emboldened by his touch, Lisa moved against him in sleek, sensual half circles. He moaned what sounded like her name, and brought his hands to her hips, pulling her against him, cupping her flesh, shaping her to the hard contours of his body.

A shrill sound came from outside their cloud of passion. They both went momentarily still. When it came again, they opened their eyes. At the third invasion, Wyatt came to his senses enough to realize that the phone was ringing.

He didn't remember moving across his kitchen or grabbing the receiver or saying "Hello," but when he was greeted by static and a voice that sounded oddly familiar, he straightened his spine and tried to pull his thoughts together.

"Yes. This is Sheriff McCully."

There was the crackle and snap of more static, more words he couldn't make out and a few that furrowed his brow.

"I've taken good...of that car, but yer lookin'...wrong places. It's under...nose. The last...you'd expect."

Wyatt knew better than to ask who it was. He only wished he could have heard more than every few words. The person on the other end of the line said something about Sugar Creek and the old Grange Hall west of town, then broke the connection.

Wyatt replaced the phone and turned around. Lisa was watching him, her eyes still warmed by passion, her lips swollen and damp from his kisses. Sending him a sassy look only she could pull off, she said, "Timing is everything, isn't it?"

Her subtle humor worked over him, adding to his need and his awe. Striding closer, he said, "Not when it's bad timing, it isn't. Whoever was on the other end of that line knows something about the whereabouts of your car. His call couldn't have come at a worse time."

"Maybe," she said, holding her ground and his gaze. "Or maybe it came in the nick of time."

She twirled around and strode to the table, where she deftly began folding the dress into a neat square and covering it with the tissue paper. Wyatt supposed he shouldn't have been surprised that his thought processes weren't working properly. A man who'd come so close to carrying a woman to his bed couldn't be expected to think straight. Lisa seemed to be having no such problem.

"It was still light outside when we got here, Wyatt. I couldn't tell you how many people turned to look as we drove by. That little old lady who was sweeping her sidewalk nearly dropped her broom when she saw me with you. If the Ladies Aid Society doesn't like me because of my past, can you imagine what a field day they'd have if I actually spent the night at your place?"

"I don't give a rip what the biddies in the Ladies Aid Society think, dammit," he declared, his voice gaining volume.

"But I do."

"You're kidding."

She shook her head. "If I ever want to fit in, in this town, I have to find a way to win the society over. And as enticing as sleeping with you sounds, I'm pretty sure that isn't the way into the hearts of the *kind* citizens of Jasper Gulch."

Wyatt raked his fingers through his hair. His patience had all but deserted him, and at this rate, his need was going to go right through the roof. But Lisa was right. She couldn't afford to be the object of any more cruel gossip, not if she wanted to find her rightful place in the community.

Suddenly he understood why she was taking such care to place the dress he'd given her in its wrapping paper. This way, anybody looking wouldn't jump to the conclusion that she'd brought a change of clothes with her. He'd lived in this small town most of his life. He knew there were drawbacks, but he would never forget the outpouring of love that had come from these people when his parents had drowned. He would never forget the welcome party they'd thrown when he'd returned from the army, either. Right now he would have traded it all for one night of anonymity in a big city.

Lisa didn't know what Wyatt was thinking. The way the muscle in his jaw was working, she didn't think it would be wise to ask. So she followed him from his house, smiling when he stepped aside and held the door for her.

She'd always thought he was light on his feet for a man his size, but there was nothing quiet about the way he slammed the back door and clanked the cover on the trash can on his way by. When he closed the truck door with a bang, then revved the engine until it sounded like a rocket about to take off, she couldn't contain her curiosity a moment longer.

Staring at his profile, she asked, "What are you doing?"

He clenched and unclenched his teeth, then slowly turned to look at her. "I'm making enough noise to bring every nosy person on this street to the window so they all know that I'm taking you home at exactly 9:45."

"Oh, Wyatt."

The muscle in his jaw relaxed, the beginning of a smile lifting one corner of his mouth. "Unless you want me to swing you into my arms and carry you back inside, you'd better not say my name that way until I've had a little time to catch my breath."

Lisa grinned when he threw the gearshift into Reverse and deftly punched on the lights. When he rammed the lever into First and stomped on the accelerator with enough force to give her whiplash, she clicked her seat belt into place and held on to her seat.

"Are you okay?" he asked.

"I'm fine," she answered, thinking that even when Wyatt was behaving like a rogue, he was a gentleman.

Lisa clipped the last article of clothing onto the clothesline in her tiny backyard then stood back to view her handiwork. It was only nine o'clock in the morning, but a warm breeze was already fluttering through the delicate wisps of satin and lace. She'd awakened humming two mornings in a row. Even the fact that she'd been her own biggest customer when she'd bought these bras and panties yesterday couldn't dampen her spirits or chase away the anticipation that had been chasing through her ever since Wyatt had given her his gift the night before last.

She'd been nearly bursting with it yesterday when Louetta came in at her usual time. Feeling fanciful and sexy, she'd decided to purchase a few undergarments, asking Louetta for her opinion on every item she chose. It had been a pleasant surprise to discover that her shy friend had extremely good taste.

Blushing to the roots of her hair, Louetta had said, "I wish I had an ounce of your courage."

Lisa had tilted her head in understanding and quietly asked, "What would you do if your wish suddenly came true?"

With her eyes fixed on the floor, Louetta had answered, "I'd make a life for myself before it's too late."

"It's never too late, Louetta," she'd said. And she'd believed it with her whole heart.

She still did. Casting another look at the garments on the clothesline, Lisa placed the empty basket in the house, then began the five-block walk to work. Since the store didn't officially open until ten, she decided to stop at the Clip & Curl on her way by.

"Good morning. Can I help you?" Bonnie Trumble, whose latest hair color was almost the same shade of orange as the front of the beauty salon, asked.

"Do you have time to trim my hair?" Lisa asked.

"Yes, yes of course, if you're sure now is a good time for you."

Lisa didn't know what to make of the warning glint in Bonnie's eyes. Following the course of the other woman's furtive glance into the back of the salon, understanding dawned. Mertyl Gentry, Opal Graham and Isabell Pruitt were openly watching her from underneath three bright pink hair dryers.

Lisa felt the color drain from her face. Her timing really was lousy. She'd needed a haircut for weeks, but had waited until this morning to get one. Not one to let a little open censure in other people's eyes intimidate her, she forced her lips into a smile and took the chair. "Just a trim, please."

Tying a cape at Lisa's neck, Bonnie went to work. Although the kindly, middle-aged beautician seemed to be doing her best to keep up a steady prattle about her husband and their grown daughter who'd moved to Rapid City right out of high school, she couldn't quite drown out the sound of the voices coming from the other side of the room.

"Did I mention that Wyatt rescued my Daisy from that big old oak tree a few weeks ago?" Mertyl Gentry asked.

"No, dear, I don't believe you did," Opal Graham answered.

"Such a nice man. I remember when he used to come into my grocery store when he was a child. He'd stand in front of the candy counter for hours, trying to decide how to spend his shiny dime. Always said please and thank you, too."

"Our Wyatt always was a polite young man," Isabell declared, her nasal voice raised over the hum of her hair dryer.

"My, yes," Opal agreed. "He still is a polite young man."

"Yes," Isabell said shrewdly. "Imagine what a shame it would be to see his sterling reputation tarnished after all this time."

"A shame. Yes, yes indeed."

Bonnie Trumble flipped the switch on her hand-held blow dryer, the sound drowning out whatever else the other women said. Lisa walked out of the shop a short time later, her hair neatly trimmed and styled. She didn't allow herself to look in the window on her way by. Although she held her head high, her mind was filled with doubts and fears. Her throat felt raw with unuttered protests. Her temples ached, and deep in her chest her heart did, too.

It had been this way when she was a child, too. Until she met Jillian and Cori and Ivy, she'd always been on the outside looking in. As a child she'd been taunted for her shabby clothes. She'd been neglected. Unloved. Years later her three closest friends had given her something nobody else ever had. They'd accepted her with open arms. They laughed with her and worried with her and loved her. An incredible feeling of homesickness washed over Lisa, making her wonder if she'd done the right thing by moving out here, after all.

She opened her store a few minutes before ten and spent the rest of the morning straightening shelves and racks that didn't really need to be straightened. She started listening for the bell over the door at 11:20. At twelve o'clock sharp she faced the fact that Louetta wasn't going to show up for her usual browse.

Opal and Isabell must have gotten to her, too.

Feeling bereft and disheartened, she locked the store and headed home for lunch. She waved at Mel through the diner's front window and called hello to a few of the Jasper Gents. She remembered Wyatt telling her it took twelve acts of kindness to make up for one negative deed. The thought of Wyatt brought a smile to her lips, but it didn't lift the heavy feeling from her heart.

"Hey, Lisa!" Jillian called, catching up with her in front of the gas station on the corner. "I'm all finished with my work at Luke's animal clinic this morning. I have to run a few errands, but they'll only take me ten minutes. Do you want to have lunch?"

Pasting a smile on her face that had Jillian furrowing her brow, Lisa said, "Sure. I'll go home and get things started."

"I was thinking more along the lines of the diner. My treat."

Lisa shook her head slowly. "If it's all the same to you, Jillian, I'd really rather eat at home."

"Is everything all right?" Jillian asked quietly.

"What could possibly be wrong?"

"I don't know," Jillian answered. "Why don't you tell me?"

"I'm fine. Really. Go run your errands. We can talk over lunch."

Jillian left, albeit reluctantly, and Lisa continued on her way. Feeling more tired than she'd felt in her entire life, she walked into her house and slowly made her way to the kitchen where she almost tripped over the clothes basket she'd left there that morning. Settling the basket on her hip, she went out the back door. Before she'd taken two steps toward the clothesline, she stopped in her tracks.

Bras and panties were no longer fluttering in the breeze. The line was bare except for clothespins. Her new lingerie was gone.

Her mind raced to find a logical explanation. Jillian couldn't have removed the items from the line. She'd already been gone when Lisa had gotten up. Besides, Jillian always removed the clothespins with the clothes. If she hadn't taken the dainty scraps of satin and lace, who had?

Lisa could see the McKenzies' wash billowing on the breeze in the yard next door. There didn't appear to be any gaps in their rows of towels and shirts and underwear, yet her line was empty. What in the world was going on?

For a moment she couldn't think. But then her mind cleared and her blood began to do a slow boil. There was a car thief loose in Jasper Gulch. And now there was a panty thief, as well. What had she done to cause someone to want to steal her car and clothes?

Nothing. She'd done nothing.

She thought she'd handled herself quite well since she'd moved to Jasper Gulch. All things considered. She hadn't flown off the handle when her car had been stolen. Although she would have liked to, she hadn't traipsed into the diner and given Isabell and Opal a piece of her mind when she'd learned they were boycotting her store. She hadn't even said a single disparaging word at the open censure in their faces and voices in the Clip & Curl this morning.

But enough was enough.

This time someone had gone too far. Somebody had

invaded her privacy, taking her *underwear* off the clothesline in her own backyard, underwear that was for sale in her store six days a week between ten and five.

If the people of Jasper Gulch thought she was going to take this sitting down, they could think again. Turning on her heel, she ducked around the side of the house and headed for the sheriff's office five blocks away.

Chapter Eight

Lisa marched down the street, a woman on a mission. She almost ran headlong into Louetta at the corner, but she didn't stick around long enough to explain. She didn't wave to Melody on her way by, or to the local bachelors who called hello as she passed. She stopped at the post office only long enough to yank the advertisement luring women to Jasper Gulch out of the window. Looking neither right nor left, she strode into the sheriff's office next door and promptly closed the door.

Three pairs of eyes turned to her, but Wyatt's gaze was the only one she sought. She pushed through the gate in the railing that divided the room, coming to a stop directly in front of his big metal desk. The newspaper clipping fluttered in her hand as she said, ''No wonder you had to advertise for women. Nobody in her right mind would come to Jasper Gulch otherwise.''

Two pairs of boots hit the floor as the Carson brothers found their feet. Wyatt rose more slowly, his heart pumping, his senses on red alert. He'd witnessed several emotions on Lisa's face these past few weeks, but he'd never seen the likes of the expression pulling at her features right now.

"Leese, what's wrong?"

"I've had it. That's what's wrong. I don't have to stay in this godforsaken town and take this."

Wyatt never would have seen the quiver in her chin if he hadn't been looking for it, but it said even more about the seriousness of the situation than her statement had. Luke and Clayt exchanged a look, glanced at Lisa, then reached for their hats and headed for the door. Another day Wyatt might have taken the time to appreciate their candor, but at that moment all he could do was stare at Lisa and wonder what the hell was going on.

The thought of her leaving held him immobile and made him choose his words very carefully. "What happened?"

He knew Lisa Markman well enough to know when she was fighting for control. Her shoulders were shaking from the battle of it right now. She flounced away from him as if she couldn't stand still another moment, only to turn at the railing and say, "What do you suppose there is about me that makes people hate me?"

Wyatt faced her across the expanse of his office. "You're asking the wrong person. As far as I'm concerned, there's nothing about you to dislike, let alone hate."

She took a shuddering breath. "Then you're in a definite minority, Wyatt."

"What makes you say that?"

She made a disparaging sound and began counting off the reasons on her fingers. "Two weeks ago somebody stole my car. Last week I learned that the members of the Ladies Aid Society are boycotting my store. Ten minutes ago I discovered that somebody has stolen bras and panties off my clothesline on the same day that Isabell Pruitt, Opal Graham and Mertyl Gentry were kind enough to let me know what a shame it would be for an honorable man like you to be dragged down in the mud by someone like me. And do you know what, Wyatt?''

A quiet rage began deep inside him. He would have taken great pleasure in arresting those old biddies for putting the hurt in Lisa's eyes. Unfortunately, narrow-mindedness wasn't against the law.

Lisa started to pace again. "They're right. Isabell and Opal and Mertyl are all right. They might be mean-spirited bigots, but they're right, about you at least. I've thought of nothing else all the way here. What's between you and me can never be more than physical. It couldn't possibly work out between us. We're total opposites. I stole food to survive, and you've never..."

"Were those bras see-through lace or black satin?"

"...had an impure thought in your life."

Wyatt took a step toward her. His eyes narrowed and his voice dipped low as he said, "I'm having one right now."

Lisa swallowed. "You are?"

Nodding, he moved closer and closer, his eyes blazing, his gaze trained on her mouth.

She took a shuddering breath and a small backward step. Wyatt followed. She took another, and so did he. And so it went, until she backed up against the railing and couldn't go any farther. Her pulse fluttered at the base of her neck, and her heart beat an uneven rhythm as she watched him take the last step. In a voice she couldn't seem to raise above a whisper, she said, "I'll sully your reputation."

Wyatt would have laughed—what kind of woman said *sully* in this day and age?—but his lips touched hers, and he couldn't have laughed if his life depended upon it. He'd kissed her before, passionately and tenderly. But this kiss was different. His lips covered hers, demanding a response that was as instinctive as it was powerful. He slid his fingers into her hair, tipping her face, holding her exactly where he wanted her. He wrapped his other arm around her back, drawing her tight to his body, molding her as close as they could be. Still, it wasn't close enough.

He felt the quiver that went through her body and the answering one that uncurled deep in his. Their mouths opened as they both gasped for air. Taking a shuddering breath, he moved his lips across her cheek and on to the delicate hollow below her ear where he whispered, "Do you still think what's between us could never be more than physical, Leese?"

Lisa pulled away far enough to be able to look into his eyes. Staring up at him, she couldn't move, not even to shake her head. What was between them *was* physical. It was also amazing, fulfilling, consuming, explosive, beautiful. She closed her eyes, wondering when her mind had turned into a danged thesaurus.

Sighing, she said, "What am I going to do with you?"

Combing his fingers through her hair, he said, "I have a few suggestions. Unfortunately this is a public office, and I have another theft to report. Now, why don't you tell me exactly what's been taken this time. Maybe if we put our heads together, we'll be able to figure out who was responsible."

She took a step to the side, his hands falling away from her shoulders. Walking toward his desk, she said, "I don't think it would be a good idea for you to get mixed up in my problems, Wyatt. The Ladies Aid Society is already boycotting my store. If they can do that on hearsay, they'll probably have a dang field day with this."

Wyatt felt a ping inside him, followed by a rousing pull on his senses that made it difficult to think or speak or move. He didn't know how it happened to other men, but in that instant, he fell in love. Maybe it was the aftereffects of that kiss, or the dawning realization that the real reason Lisa had tried to put a stop to what was happening between them was to save his reputation. Or maybe it was because she said *dang.* Not *damn,* not even *darn.* Dang.

He was in love, really and truly in love. He wanted to shout it, sing it, whisper it in her ear, but now was hardly the time for such declarations. She'd intimated that she might not stay in this "godforsaken" town. The thought was gut-wrenching, and filled him with the need to hit something. And that rarely happened to him.

If he could, he'd arrest Isabell, Opal and Mertyl for making Lisa feel like a tarnished woman. He'd at least like to wring the old biddies' fool necks. But right now he had more important things to do. He had to figure out which of the Jasper townsfolk stole her car, and who was perverted enough to take her underwear. And somewhere in the midst of all that, he had to find a way to tell Lisa he loved her and convince her to spend the rest of her life with him.

"Would you describe the items missing from your line?" he asked, his voice husky despite his resolve to regain at least a portion of his former professionalism.

"You've seen them."

"I don't think so, Lisa. That's hardly something I'd forget."

He looked at her, and she looked at him. She was the first to smile.

She sashayed closer, shaking her head slowly all the while. "It's not what you're thinking. You saw them in the store. You remember, don't you? You were talking to Clayt on the phone and Haley was looking at the display of lingerie."

"Haley?"

They both went perfectly still. When Wyatt moved, it was to rake a hand through his hair.

"Do you think Haley could have done it?" Lisa asked.

Wyatt's thoughts spun away to the previous month when Luke had caught Haley stealing food off Jillian's and Lisa's porch. It had only been a week since the little urchin had taken Jeremy Everts's clothes. And she had shown quite an interest in the scraps of satin and lace that day she was in the store. If Haley had taken Lisa's underclothes, it would let the Jasper Gents off the hook. But Wyatt didn't know what the knowledge would do to Clayt.

Releasing a loud breath, he said, "I'll have to question her."

"Maybe she's been miles away all day," Lisa said.

Wyatt shook his head. "She's been at Amanda Tucker's house over on Custer Street all morning. Clayt was going to pick them both up at the library a few minutes ago. I might be able to catch them before they leave, but I don't know what I'm going to say to Clayt."

"I'll go with you."

Reaching for his white cowboy hat, Wyatt followed Lisa out the door.

"Uh-oh," Haley said solemnly. "Something's going on. Something bad. Uncle Wyatt and my dad both have that look."

Lisa glanced at the two men who were talking in earnest whispers several feet away, then down at Haley who was looking more scared by the second. All Lisa could do was hope and pray that Haley had a good alibi.

She smoothed her hand down the child's light brown hair. Although Haley didn't flinch, she didn't take her eyes off her father's dark expression.

Wyatt and Clayt finished talking and strode to the library steps where Lisa and Haley were sitting. "Haley," Clayt said to his daughter, "Wyatt has a few questions he wants to ask you."

"Am I under arrest, Uncle Wyatt?"

Clayt Carson went noticeably pale beneath his dusty brown Stetson.

Turning accusing eyes to Lisa, the little girl said, "Did you tell?"

"No, Haley," Lisa said softly. "I didn't tell. When I

make a promise, I keep it. I haven't told anybody about our secret, and I won't. This is about something else, but you're definitely not under arrest. Sometime this morning somebody took some of my clothes off my clothesline, and we just want to know if you happened to be in the neighborhood.''

"Were you, Haley?" Wyatt asked, taking over.

The girl shook her head one time.

"Maybe you saw somebody lurking around."

"How could I see somebody lurking around when I was at Jeremy's house all morning?" Haley asked indignantly.

"I dropped you off at Amanda Tucker's house," Clayt said, his voice ominously low. "Not Jeremy Everts's."

Haley stuck her tongue out at the mention of the little girl's name.

"Are you saying that you snuck over to Jeremy's house without telling me?" Clayt asked.

Shading her eyes with one hand, Lisa studied Clayt and Wyatt. The hot noon sun glared off their chests, reflecting off Wyatt's silver badge. Their cowboy hats shaded their faces, but they didn't stop the beads of sweat trailing down their temples and disappearing inside the collar of their shirts.

"Haley," Clayt said, "why didn't you stay to play with Amanda?"

Suddenly the little girl seemed inordinately interested in the toe of her worn canvas shoe. "Amanda's a sissy. She's afraid of spiders and the dark and just about everything cool. Besides, she hates me. All the girls do."

Clayt started forward, but Wyatt held out a hand, stopping him in his tracks. "Then you didn't remove anything from Lisa's clothesline?" he asked.

"Of course not. What was stolen, anyway?"

Lisa glanced up at Wyatt, who was staring at her, stricken. Thinking it was amazing that a man who could climb onto the back of a bucking bronco without batting an eye couldn't seem to bring himself to talk about women's lingerie, she answered, "Some of my pretty bras and panties are missing."

Haley's eyes grew round, her mouth shaped around a silent *oh*. Jumping to her feet, she cried, "I didn't take them, honest. I didn't do it, I didn't. Cross my heart and hope to die."

"I believe you."

"You can even ask Jeremy. He'll tell you—" Haley's head jerked around. "What did you say?"

Lisa stood. Taking Haley's chin in her hand, she said, "I believe you."

"You do?"

Lisa nodded, and Clayt mumbled, "Thank God."

Haley pulled her chin out of Lisa's grasp and looked up at her father. "Do you believe me, too, Daddy?"

Clayt went down on his haunches. When he nodded, Lisa knew she was witnessing an important moment between a father and his daughter.

Clayt and Haley left seconds later. Watching them go, Lisa said, "I'm glad she didn't do it."

"You're quite a woman."

The depth of feeling in Wyatt's voice drew Lisa around to face him. With a slow, secret smile she said, "You've said that before."

"I know what I'm talking about."

She wondered when Wyatt McCully had acquired his arrogant streak. In anyone else it would have been exasperating, but in him it was amazingly endearing.

His expression was always filled with intensity, but it had a way of changing before her very eyes when he was thinking about kissing her. It was happening right now. It left her feeling warm and wanted, feminine, cherished almost.

The shadow of his hat made his eyes appear darker, but it didn't detract from the open look of longing or the hon-

est affection in his gaze. Men rarely tried to disguise their
desire for her, and Wyatt was no exception. But she'd
never met anyone who let his respect and regard shine for
all to see. Only Wyatt did that.

Brakes squealed at the corner, and voices called to one
another down the street, reminding them that they were on
the town's busiest street. Lisa had a sudden, burning wish
that they were someplace else, all alone.

Wyatt ambled closer. "I like what you're thinking."

"How do you know what I'm thinking?"

He smiled, and Lisa slowly shook her head. She didn't
know how much longer her heart could stand being pum-
meled with kindness. She didn't know how much longer
the rest of her could stand being wanted by a man like
Wyatt McCully.

Tipping her head slightly, she said, "You know this puts
us back to square one."

He pushed at the brim of his hat and said, "With the
case, maybe. But not when it comes to us."

He leaned toward her and kissed her right there on the
town's main street. The kiss didn't last long, but it was
enough to send her thoughts to the other side of the moon.
He raised his face from hers, and danged if he didn't grin.
Giving his hat a tug, he said, "I'll see you after work. I,
for one, can hardly wait."

It wasn't easy to pull her gaze away from him as he
walked away. Wyatt McCully had a masculine swagger
that was difficult to ignore. The quick glance over his
shoulder and his subsequent grin told her that he knew it.
Lisa didn't know what to do about the emotion clamoring
inside her. She was afraid to call it love, and was at a loss
to call it anything else. Whatever it was, it made her heart
feel two sizes larger, and her spirits soar.

Maybe she'd been wrong about her chance at happiness
here in Jasper Gulch. Maybe she'd been wrong about the
kind of man she was looking for, too. Maybe all her hopes

and dreams were waiting for her behind a pair of golden brown eyes and a shiny silver badge.

A movement at the top of the library steps drew her gaze. She had a smile all ready for Louetta, who worked in the library, but came face-to-face with Isabell Pruitt's stony glare instead. No one had ever accused Lisa of being sweet. Still, she couldn't help smiling at the other woman.

Isabell raised what little chin she had and haughtily turned away. Lisa accepted the snub for what it was and headed for her house on Elm Street where Jillian was waiting for lunch.

Anyone looking had probably noticed the change in her step, but nobody could have known the reason she suddenly felt so light on her feet. Wyatt thought she was an incredible woman, and she was beginning to believe him.

She winked at Jason Tucker on her way by and smiled to herself when he blushed. She really had no idea what she was going to do about her clothing store. Strangely, it didn't seem like such a big problem. She didn't even bother to glance over her shoulder when a catcall rent the air, and she certainly didn't cringe. Why should she? She was falling in love. And she didn't think there was anything anybody could do to chase away these hopes and dreams filling her heart and soul today.

Headlights flickered across the dry prairie grass lining the highway. A country-western ballad played softly over the radio. Lisa felt relaxed and more comfortable than she ever could have imagined. Sitting next to Wyatt in his old pickup truck, she remembered when he'd told her he couldn't carry a tune in a basket. That may have been so, but his hum was mellow and deep and masculine, and brought a sense of intimacy to the darkness.

She'd thought there was nothing that could speed up her heart faster than a man wearing a cowboy hat and chaps, but she'd taken one look at Wyatt when he'd walked into the diner just before quitting time, and every preconceived notion she'd ever had of what constituted a rugged, handsome man disappeared into thin air. He was wearing a white dress shirt, open at the neck, and dark gray pants slung low on his hips. His hair looked freshly combed, his face clean shaven. His cowboy hat was nowhere to be found, which proved that it wasn't the trappings that made a man rugged.

They were on their way back to Jasper Gulch after having a late dinner in Pierre. It was their first real date, and she suspected that he'd been on his best behavior, holding doors, pushing in chairs, listening intently to every word she said. His eyes alone had betrayed his ardor, straying below her shoulders, glimmering with longing and need and desire.

She wasn't sure why she'd changed her clothes after filling Jillian in on the latest happenings at lunchtime, but she'd gone back to the store feeling refreshed, almost carefree in one of the dresses she'd brought with her from Madison. She was saving the pale blue dress Wyatt had given her to wear to the barbecue on Saturday, and from now on, she wasn't going to limit her clothing to the Western wear she sold in her store. She wasn't giving up, and she certainly didn't plan to go away, but she was going to wear what she liked. And tonight she was glad she'd chosen this soft green dress. The way the fabric followed her curves, cinched in at her waist and hugged her hips made her feel feminine and whimsical and alluring.

Or was Wyatt responsible for that?

He pulled the truck to a stop at the curb in front of her house. Lisa knew he would have opened her door for her if she'd let him, but there was no way she could contain the giddy sense of anticipation inside her long enough to wait for him to round the front of the truck. She slipped out of the passenger door and faced him on the grassy slope of her small front yard.

Wyatt slowed his steps, coming to a complete standstill directly in front of Lisa. The wind blew her hair across her face and fluttered the hem of her dress against his knees. Laughing, she caught her hair in one hand, the movement so lithe and winsome it made him ache. Lisa had always been sultry and warm and more than a little brash, but there was something different about her tonight. Her smiles were a little softer, her gaze a little brighter, her sighs a little deeper.

Leaning closer so that she could hear his whisper, he said, "I think you and I are the only two people awake in all of Jasper Gulch tonight."

She placed one hand over his heart and looked up at him. The porch light was too far away to penetrate the darkness, the stars too faint, which meant that the glimmer in her dark brown eyes was coming from within. He wondered if she could feel his heart speed up beneath her palm. Lowering his face to hers, he hoped so. He wanted her to know the effect she was having on his body.

He knew before his lips touched hers that a kiss would never be enough, but he moved his mouth over hers, anyway, devouring its softness. She kissed him back, her lips urgent, exploratory and so eager it took his breath away. If they hadn't had a silly, nonsensical need for oxygen, the kiss might have gone on forever. Dragging in deep breaths, they took turns smiling and shaking their heads. By unspoken consent they began to make their way to her front porch.

They walked up the steps together, but Wyatt stopped a few feet from the door. She turned to look at him, one hand on the screen's latch. "Aren't you going to come in?"

He shook his head. "I'm afraid I don't have that much self-control. And you deserve a man who can do the honorable thing."

Lisa swallowed, her heart beating a rhythm so heavy

she was certain it would drop lower in her chest. No man had ever made her feel so virtuous. No man had ever made her want him more.

He kissed her again, his lips brushing gently over hers before he turned and strode away. She watched him climb into his truck and lifted her hand to return his wave moments before he pulled away. She stared out into the night for a long time after he left, smiling.

She closed the door after a while, and turned out the lamp Jillian had left on for her, then quietly made her way up the narrow flight of stairs. Light shone through the gap beneath the door at the end of the hall. Instead of entering her bedroom, she tiptoed to Jillian's room and pressed her hand against the old-fashioned, raised-panel door. The hinges creaked slightly as the door slowly opened.

She did a double take when Jillian smiled from the other side of the room. The lamp cast an ethereal glow on Jillian's wedding gown, giving her hair a darker luster and her skin a pale hue.

Striking a pose that went all the way back to the early days of their friendship, Lisa said, "For a minute I thought you were an angel. But I guess I should have known better, huh?"

Jillian threw a pillow at her. When Lisa caught it easily, Jillian said, "Tell me the truth. How do I look?"

Wrapping her arms around the pale yellow pillow, Lisa whispered, "Oh, Jillian, you look beautiful, absolutely beautiful. But I thought you'd be asleep. What are you doing trying on your wedding dress at one o'clock in the morning?"

Turning back to the mirror, Jillian said, "I keep imagining that I'm walking down the aisle where the man I love is waiting for me. Only me."

"Oh, Jillian."

Jillian Daniels stopped toying with the gathers in her

gown and stared at Lisa through the mirror. "Is it my imagination, or are you really floating?"

Lisa did a double take all over again. Even after all these years, Jillian had the ability to surprise her. Tossing the pillow to a chair, Lisa plopped down on the foot of the bed only to bounce back onto her feet seconds later. "Have you ever felt as if everything that's ever happened in your entire life has led to this exact moment in time?"

Jillian lowered the zipper on the back of the dress, then turned to face Lisa once again. "I've felt that way ever since I caught the bouquet at Cori's wedding last month."

"Maybe I'll catch the bouquet at yours," Lisa whispered.

"Maybe we should make it a double wedding."

Lisa's head came up and around, her mouth gaping, her eyes open wide. Recovering slightly, she said, "Wyatt hasn't asked me to marry him."

"So?"

"What do you mean, 'so'?" Lisa asked. "You think *I* should ask *him?*"

Pulling her arm out of one long, lacy sleeve, Jillian arched her sleek auburn eyebrows and said, "Why not? I asked Luke."

"You did?"

Jillian nodded conspiratorially. "Sometimes a woman has to do what a woman has to do."

Staring at the red-haired woman who'd been her best friend for more than half her life, Lisa's thoughts spun with possibilities. "I don't know, Jillian," she said after a brief silence. "I don't want to rush into anything. Right now, I just want to enjoy these incredible feelings deep inside me."

Jillian nodded in understanding. "If it's in the stars, it'll happen, just wait and see."

Lisa didn't even bother scoffing at Jillian's belief in astrology and astronomy and fates sealed in the stars. Turning, she said, "Good night, Jillian."

Jillian called good-night, and Lisa strode to the tiny bathroom where she washed her face and brushed her teeth and tried to imagine Wyatt's expression should she decide to take Jillian's advice.

Crawling into bed, she thought what a difference time could make. A few months ago she'd begun to wonder if this kind of happiness was meant for other people. And then she'd met Wyatt, and as hard as she'd fought it, she'd fallen in love. She was pretty sure he was falling in love with her, too. No man would sacrifice his own need for a woman's well-being unless he cared for her on some deep, heartfelt level.

Once again airy hopes filled her mind and her senses. Closing her eyes, she couldn't think of anything that could chase away the powerful feelings inside her. With Wyatt's smile dallying around the edges of her mind, she slowly drifted off to sleep where she dreamed about double weddings and marriage proposals and wishes that came true.

Wyatt hiked his boot onto the corner of Cletus's favorite bench. Cletus snapped his suspender, and Clayt tipped the brim of his hat as he looked up at him, but neither of them said anything about his inane grin. Wyatt wouldn't have cared if they had. After all, he was feeling pretty darned good. Incredible—that's what he was feeling—invigorated, invincible. He was a little surprised he wasn't dog tired, what with the amount of sleep he'd gotten last night. He'd finally drifted off sometime after two a.m., only to wake up at the break of dawn, the sheets a tangled heap at his feet. Strangely, he'd never felt better. Whoever said love was grand had known what he was talking about.

Cletus grinned when Haley slurped the last of the soda her father had bought for her at the gas station on the

corner, and Clayt said, "Oh, oh, here comes old Olive
Oyl."

Wyatt thought Haley's giggle was a good sign that she
was recovering from her mother's abandonment. As far as
he could tell, she was losing her ragamuffin appearance.
Her hair was neatly combed today, and her shorts and
T-shirt lacked their usual grass stains. The little girl was
bouncing back, and he was glad.

He took a deep breath, enjoying the feeling of rightness
that settled around him. Everything was going to work out.
The drought was over, Luke had found a bride, and Wyatt
had found Lisa.

"Gentlemen," Isabell declared, flouncing directly in
front of Cletus's favorite bench.

"Afternoon, Isabell," Cletus said with a wink that
earned him an indignant huff.

It looked as if old Isabell had a bee in her bonnet again.
Wondering what she was all fired up about this time, Wyatt
lowered his foot to the sidewalk and squared his shoulders.

"I called a special meeting of the Ladies Aid Society
earlier this afternoon," Isabell began. "And with a unan-
imous vote it was decided that someone simply had to
speak up. Naturally, I was elected to carry out this trying
task."

An ominous sense of foreboding crawled down Wyatt's
spine, but Cletus was the first to find his voice. "This ain't
hardly the time or the place, Isabell."

The warning in Cletus's voice only fueled Isabell's ir-
ritation. She shifted indignantly from one foot to the other
and took turns pointing her finger at Clayt and Wyatt. "As
members of the town council, you two young men are
leaders of our community. You have a moral obligation to
set a good example for our young and old alike."

Staring at Clayt, she said, "You should be ashamed of
yourself, letting your daughter run wild. Why, every book
I've ever read about parenting clearly states that a child

needs discipline. It's bad enough that Haley stole food. But women's underwear! Why, it's positively reprehensible."

Isabell didn't so much as bat an eye when Haley tried to defend herself. She simply raised her voice and continued. "Reprehensible, but completely understandable. Why, I'm not surprised an impressionable child took it upon herself to steal such things from a woman like that."

Clayt rose to his feet. His eyes were narrowed, his expression severe, that old Carson temper mere seconds away from igniting and blowing up in Isabell's face. "Haley said she didn't do it," he ground out. "And I believe her."

Isabell continued as if he hadn't spoken. "Now, Clayton, I'm not really blaming you. The way that, that *hussy* walks and carries on invites trouble. Haley probably couldn't help herself. But, Clayton, you really should consider boarding school for that child."

Wyatt's insides twisted in anger, his hands squeezing into fists at his sides. "That's enough, Isabell," he said, his voice practically a growl. "Didn't anyone ever teach you that it wasn't polite to call people names? And for the record, I happen to believe Haley, too."

Isabell appeared genuinely surprised by the reprimand. Recovering, she jutted out her pointed little chin and said, "Pardon me, Sheriff, if I'm having a difficult time trusting your judgment these days. Maybe you should think about what someone like that Markman woman would do to your chances of being reelected next year. Or were you thinking about running for *dogcatcher* the next time around?"

Cletus rose to his feet and stood as tall as his stoop-shouldered frame would allow. Peering beneath bushy white eyebrows, he said, "You listen here, you old battle-ax. I've put up with your meddling all my life, but you just went too far. I've never hit a woman, and I ain't about to start now. But either you button your lip or I'll button it for you."

Old Isabell took a small step backward. Her bony hands

clutched her shiny white purse, shaking slightly as she said, "Well, I never!"

"Yeah?" Cletus growled. "I'd say that's your problem."

Wyatt had never been more proud of his grandfather in his life. Isabell gave an affronted huff, raised her chin and flounced away, her flat-soled shoes slapping on the sidewalk with every step she took.

Haley was crying, and Clayt was fuming, and Cletus was sputtering. Just when Wyatt thought things couldn't get any worse, he looked up, straight into Lisa's eyes twenty feet away.

Chapter Nine

Although Wyatt couldn't see the expression in Lisa's eyes clearly from this distance, he read her body language loud and clear. She was standing in front of the library, her shoulders squared, her back straight. She held her head high, although that alone seemed to require a great deal of effort. She drew in a shaky breath, then slowly turned away.

"Lisa, wait!" Wyatt shouted, hurrying after her.

She came to a stop with stiff dignity. When she raised her gaze to his, there was so much caution in her eyes he was at a loss for words. He didn't know how long she'd been standing there, but it was obvious she'd heard enough. Too much, dammit.

Keeping his voice as controlled as possible, he said, "Don't pay any attention to—"

She held up one hand, stopping him in the middle of what he'd been about to say. After lowering her hand to her side, she stood motionless in the middle of the sidewalk, her eyes trained on him, the wind ruffling her hair and toying with the collar of her sleeveless denim shirt.

Wyatt could feel eyes on them from every direction, but he was the most aware of the gaping stares coming from the group of gray-haired women huddled together at the end of the block, cackling like wet hens in a crowded chicken coop.

Lisa seemed to be doing everything in her power to hold on to her composure. Her mouth was set in a straight line, her features controlled. Whether she knew it or not, she wasn't hiding the hurt glittering in her eyes.

"Believe me, Wyatt," she said quietly. "I've been called worse names than *hussy*."

The knowledge didn't make him feel any better, but before he could do more than take an abrupt step toward her, a horn honked, an engine roared, and somebody yelled, "Hit the brake, Roy! Not the gas. The brake!"

Wyatt and Lisa both swung around in time to see Roy Everts's rusty Chevrolet jump the curb in front of Ed's Barbershop across the street. The old-timers who were sitting on the bench underneath the red-and-white barber pole scattered seconds before the sound of splintering wood rent the air.

Wyatt braced himself for the sound of walls crashing and glass breaking. When it became apparent that Roy had managed to stop his car before those things could happen, Wyatt glanced back at Lisa. "I don't want to, but I have to go. We'll talk later, okay?"

"Don't worry about me, Wyatt. I'll be fine."

He wasn't so sure about that. The last thing he wanted to do was leave her, but he didn't have much choice. He sprinted across the street, assessing the situation in one sweeping glance. Doc Masey and Karl Hanson were standing on one side of the car, and Jed Harely and Forest Wilkie were leaning on their canes on the other side. The only damage appeared to be to the wooden bench lying in a broken heap underneath Roy's bumper.

Catching sight of Lisa as she walked away, Wyatt had

to wonder how much damage had been done to her. He was proud of the way she'd handled the criticism of some of the residents in this town, but he didn't know how much more she could withstand.

Everybody started talking at once. The folks of Jasper Gulch had grown accustomed to the way Roy Everts took out mailboxes and fence posts with the bumper of his old car, but this was the first time he'd nearly crashed through the front of the barbershop and into four of his best friends.

Roy apologized up one side and down the other. It seemed he'd been so busy watching the little scene taking place near Cletus's bench he'd forgotten to pay attention to what he was doing and had hit the accelerator instead of the brake. Although Wyatt did his best to remain focused on the situation at hand, the memory of the hurt in Lisa's eyes was never far from his mind. He wrote down the necessary information, issued Roy a ticket, then headed straight for the Jasper Gulch Clothing Store. He took a little satisfaction in ducking around the group of women of the Ladies Aid Society, thereby giving them something else to gossip about. But his revenge was short-lived.

A Closed sign was hanging in the clothing store's window, and the door was locked tight.

He didn't like the dull ache of foreboding filling his chest, but the raw panic lengthening his stride was even worse. He didn't know what he was going to do, but he had to find Lisa before it was too late.

Wyatt pulled the sheriff's car to a stop and opened the door. Other than a handful of cars and trucks parked underneath the streetlight in front of the town's only bar, Main Street was deserted. He remembered when the awning over his sister's diner had been bright red. Years of sun, dust and weather had faded it to its present dullness. The entire business district of Jasper Gulch was a block long and was made up of painted brick buildings the color of sand. The pink flowers Lisa had planted next to her store's front door brightened an otherwise drab street. The same could be said for Lisa. She'd moved into town two months ago, her flirty walk fueling his fantasies, her dark brown hair and laughing eyes coloring his world. Could he really be the only person in town to see it?

He wasn't sure why he'd come back to the Crazy Horse. All he knew was that he'd run out of places to look. He'd tried Lisa's store, the diner, her house on Elm Street. He'd checked with Mel, who'd given Lisa the night off, and he'd spoken with Jillian and Luke and Cletus and everybody else he could think of who might know where she'd gone. Everyone's answer was the same. Nobody had seen her since four o'clock that afternoon.

The dull ache of foreboding in his chest was steadily growing into a monster-size worry. Jillian had done her best to reassure him. To no avail. It was true that Lisa didn't have a car, and Jasper Gulch wasn't exactly the kind of place that offered public transportation. The nearest airports and train stations were miles away. Wyatt kept telling himself that Lisa wouldn't just up and leave, but his gut instinct said she might.

Who could blame her?

He dragged his hat off his head and raked his fingers through his hair, then stood in the doorway, hat in hand, peering into the bar's hazy interior, where a few of the Thursday night regulars were playing poker. The sight of Boomer Brown cozying up to DoraLee was commonplace these days, and Wyatt had heard the song about "forever and ever, amen" playing on the jukebox a hundred times. But it was the sight of the woman sitting all alone in the back of the room that caused him to draw his first easy breath in hours. Lisa Markman was a sight for sore eyes. She had been since the moment he first saw her.

DoraLee caught his attention, gesturing for him to come closer. She plunked a cold bottle of beer in front of him before he'd taken the stool next to Boomer. "How long has she been here, DoraLee?"

The bleached-blond proprietor of the Crazy Horse shook her head and quietly said, "Twenty minutes, half an hour at the most. She's been sittin' there as quiet as a mouse, staring into the same soda ever since she took a seat at that table. I tried talking to her, and she tried smilin', but she couldn't quite pull it off. That girl's hurting. Sugar, you've gotta do something."

Keeping his eyes trained on the mirror behind the bar, Wyatt took a long swig from the ice-cold bottle in front of him. He dropped a bill on the counter and turned, slowly making his way to the back of the room.

A hush had fallen over the bar. Lisa knew without looking that Wyatt was heading her way. She waited to lift her eyes to his until after he'd placed his bottle of beer on the table and took the chair opposite her.

"Can I buy you another drink?"

She shook her head.

"In that case, how about letting me give you a ride home?"

She stared at him, thinking. He was still wearing his uniform, but not his badge. His shirt was wrinkled, the top two buttons undone, his face in need of a shave. There were small lines next to his eyes, a deeper one creasing one lean cheek. He looked as if he'd been pulled through a knothole backward. As far as she was concerned, no man had ever looked better.

"You're not an easy woman to track down."

She shrugged. "I haven't been hiding, if that's what you're thinking."

"That wasn't what I was thinking."

The deep timbre in Wyatt's voice sent an ache to Lisa's already throbbing temples. Leave it to him to think the best of her no matter what. He'd probably been searching frantically for her. She was sorry if she'd caused him to worry. She'd taken a long walk out to Sugar Creek because she'd needed to be alone. She'd needed to think. And that's exactly what she'd done. Lord, she was tired, but things were a lot clearer now. And she knew what she had to do.

Although she had some truly wonderful friends, she'd faced the world alone most of her life, at the mercy of fate and the powers that be. She'd been hurt, but she'd survived, her very existence making her strong. Isabell Pruitt's incriminations had felt like a slap in the face, but she'd recovered. If she'd had no one to think about other than herself, she'd make a scene and tell the old spinster exactly what she thought of her. But there was more at stake here than her own reputation. Wyatt's future was on the line, and Lisa simply couldn't take a chance with that.

She reached into her pocket for one of the dollar bills she'd received in tips. Flattening it to the table, she rose to her feet.

"I must have walked five miles tonight. I'd appreciate a ride home."

He was around the table before she could blink. His hand felt warm where he cupped her elbow and steered her around the chairs blocking their path. It was all she could do to keep from melting into his side. But she couldn't do that. For his sake, she had to be strong a little longer.

Wyatt drove through the quiet streets of his hometown, being careful not to turn the corners too sharply. Lisa leaned against the passenger door, looking more fragile than he'd ever seen her. He carried on a one-sided conversation all the way to her house, telling her about some of the good people of Jasper Gulch and about some of his fondest memories. He thought she almost smiled when he told her how Mel had kicked Clayt in the shins when she was seven years old, but by the time he'd pulled the truck to a stop in front of her house, her mouth was set in a straight line once again.

Jillian and Luke jumped to their feet the instant they set foot in the house. "Oh, Lisa, thank God you're back." Her friend asked, "Are you all right?"

"I'm fine. You know I always bounce back." Her voice lacked its usual vehemence, and her wink looked out of place on her own face.

It was obvious that Jillian wanted to stay, but Luke must have read the look Wyatt shot at him, because within seconds he took Jillian's hand and drew her out to his truck on the pretense of going for a drive and looking at the stars.

With a shake of her head and a smile that didn't quite reach her eyes, Lisa said, "Luke isn't exactly the most subtle man on the planet, is he?"

Wyatt tossed his hat to the back of a wooden rocking chair and shook his head. Rotating a kink out of his shoulders, he said, "I remember one time when we were, oh, maybe twelve years old, Luke and I—"

He stopped suddenly. When she looked up at him, he started toward her, saying, "It just occurred to me that I've been doing all the talking tonight. What about you, Leese? Don't you have something you want to say?"

Wyatt didn't like the lethal calmness in her eyes, or the way she shrugged then slowly turned away. "In all honesty, I wouldn't know where to begin."

She strode to the kitchen. He followed as far as the doorway. Leaning against the curved archway, he said, "I've been talking about memories. Why don't you tell me about a few of yours?"

She measured him for so long he wondered if she planned to answer. After a time, she leaned down and removed a watering can from underneath the sink. Inspecting one of the many plants on the windowsill, she said, "This soil is dry as a bone."

She tipped up the watering can, then moved on to the ivy plant hanging over the sink. Wyatt folded his arms at his chest. And waited.

Finally she said, "I don't have a lot of memories of my childhood."

"Surely you must have a few. What would you say is your most vivid memory?"

"My most vivid memory," she said, watering a fern on the counter. "Let's see. That would either be my first kiss..."

Wyatt straightened and made a derisive snort.

"Or the day my father went to prison. I'll never forget that day, or the slap my mother's latest boyfriend gave me for crying."

Wyatt's throat constricted. Letting his instincts guide him, he strolled forward with long, purposeful strides. Lisa might have been trying to appear nonchalant, but the water running over the saucer beneath the rhododendron gave her away. He reached for a towel and took her by the hand.

She looked up at him, and he swore he'd never seen so much intensity in a woman's eyes. "I told you I'm not much for memories," she said, fighting valiantly to smile.

Luke and Clayt had always been the ones to raise their fists. Staring at the dark smudges beneath Lisa's eyes and the dark emotions inside them, he wouldn't have minded five minutes alone with the man who'd slapped her all those years ago. He knew such a wish was futile, but in that instant he would have done anything to take away the haunted look in her eyes.

"Remember this," he whispered, lowering his face to hers.

She kept her eyes open, and so did he, his vision blurring slightly, his thoughts hazy. And then, as if connected to the same heartstrings, their eyelids drifted down, and they both sighed.

Wyatt slipped his arms around her back, drawing her

closer. Taking great care to keep the kiss tender, he raised his face from hers. Pressing his lips to the top of her head, he murmured, "Ah, this feels good. *You* feel good."

She pulled away a few inches and said, "Wyatt, there's something I have to tell you."

Call it gut instinct, call it intuition, call it fear, but a primitive warning sounded in Wyatt's brain. He didn't know where the sudden burning need to kiss her again came from, but he knew what to do about it. He lowered his face to hers, covering her mouth with his in a kiss that was far from gentle.

She made a sound deep in her throat and kissed him back, sending the pit of his stomach into a wild swirl. Before the kiss had gone nearly far enough, he felt her stiffen and knew she was about to pull away. Reluctantly he let her go.

Taking a backward step out of his arms, she asked, "Why did you do that?"

"Since when does a man need a reason to kiss a woman?"

Lisa took a shuddering breath and closed her eyes. This was going to be even harder than she'd thought. She replaced the watering can, using the time it took to open and close the cupboard door to get her thoughts in order. By the time she'd straightened, her voice was much more composed. "There's something you should know."

"What?" he asked. "That there's scandal in your past? That you ran away from home, and your father went to prison, and you had to take desperate measures to survive? I don't care. The past is past. I'm more interested in today. And tomorrow."

She walked to the window where she pushed aside the gauzy curtain and peered out into the darkness. She could see the McKenzies' nightlight from here. Although the children said please and thank you whenever she returned a ball that had landed in her yard, she'd never had a real conversation with their parents or with any of the other adults on this street for that matter. Maybe she didn't belong here.

She had no ties to this town or to any town. Her ties were to people. And the people of Jasper Gulch didn't want her. Who in her right mind would want to stay in such a place?

She did. Because Wyatt was here.

Everything she'd ever dreamed of was standing right behind her. It would have been so easy to give in to the nearly overwhelming yearning to walk back into his arms and stay there until morning. But she couldn't do that.

Wyatt McCully was the most honorable man she'd ever met. Although he hadn't said it in so many words, his roots in Jasper Gulch went as deep as his integrity. His voice was always filled with intensity, but never more than when he regaled her with stories of the people in this town. He'd been born here. He'd come back here after his brief stint in the army. And he would grow old here.

Isabell Pruitt might have had the lips of a chicken, but she was right about Wyatt's reputation. If she had enough power to persuade the members of the Ladies Aid Society to boycott the Jasper Gulch Clothing Store, Lisa had little doubt that she could see to it that Wyatt wasn't elected sheriff of Jones County next year.

Lisa wasn't a novice at doing the right thing. It was just that the right thing had never been more difficult to do than at this moment.

"Look," Wyatt said, his voice coming from little more than a foot behind her. "It's been a long, trying day. It's no wonder you're exhausted. Everything will look brighter in the morning after you've had a good night's sleep. You'll see. And in two weeks this will all be just another distant memory."

"Two weeks won't change the fact that we're complete opposites," she said quietly.

"I'm a man and you're a woman. It doesn't get much more opposite than that."

She let go of the curtain, but she didn't turn around. "I'm thinking about going back to Madison."

There. She'd said it. It hadn't been easy, but she'd said it.

"What? When?"

"Soon."

That one small word shimmered through Wyatt's mind, dropping to his chest and spreading outward like a ripple on a glass-smooth lake. Lisa was thinking about leaving. Soon.

Damn.

He stared at her profile, unmoving. And then he slowly raised his hand to her cheek. She leaned into his touch for a moment, then pulled away.

"I don't want to fight with the Ladies Aid Society, Wyatt. I don't want to hurt anybody. Especially you. Please don't make this any more difficult than it is."

Her request was still hanging in the air between them when a knock sounded on the front door. Before he and Lisa could do more than turn around, the door was jerked open and Clayt Carson strode into the kitchen.

"Wyatt, we have to do something. I've looked everywhere. And I can't find her."

"Who?" Wyatt asked. "Who can't you find?"

"Haley. I can't find Haley. My little girl is gone!"

Chapter Ten

"Tell me what happened, Clayt."

Wyatt's voice sounded loud in his own ears, every nerve in his body on the alert. He thought he'd seen every expression in the book on his friend's face, but nothing he'd ever seen came close to the dread and the fear in Clayt's eyes right now.

Raking a hand through his dark hair, Clayt said, "She was weepy and tired after we got home this afternoon. She kept asking me why nobody likes her and if I was going to send her to boarding school like Isabell said. I told her I loved her and would never dream of sending her away."

"What did she say to that?" Wyatt asked.

"Not much. I thought it was a good sign when she calmed down and informed me that she was going out to the barn to pet the new kittens. When I called her in for supper half an hour later, she didn't come. At first I figured she'd probably fallen asleep, so I went out to wake her, expecting to find her curled up with the mother cat and all six kittens. But she wasn't there. I've looked everywhere,

Wyatt, in her room, under the bed, in the barn, behind the shed. She's gone. My little girl is gone."

"Do you think she ran away?" Lisa asked.

For a moment Clayt seemed surprised that Lisa was there. Glancing around as if coming out of a daze, he nodded. A muscle worked in his jaw, and he went noticeably pale.

"Did she take anything with her?" Lisa asked. "Anything from her room? A change of clothes, maybe, or food?"

Wyatt doubted that Clayt was in any condition to appreciate the way Lisa had sauntered closer and lowered her voice to a soothing level, but he'd never forget it. For the life of him, he didn't know how the people of Jasper Gulch could be so blind to her goodness.

"As far as I can tell," Clayt answered, "the only things Haley took were the clothes on her back, a package of drink boxes, a box of crackers and the blanket she dragged everywhere when she was two."

Turning to Wyatt, Clayt said, "It's the last day of August, and the nights are already getting cooler. She's out there somewhere, all alone. And she's only nine years old."

Wyatt clasped his friend's shoulder with one hand. "We'll find her, Clayt. She's a tough little kid. Don't forget how she rode her bike two miles into town and back again—in the dark—those nights she took food off Lisa's front porch. She knows how to take care of herself. She's a Carson."

Although Clayt's attitude remained tense, he took a deep breath and visibly pulled himself together. "I have to find her. But I'll need help."

"You've already got it," Wyatt said. "Luke went for a drive with Jillian, but they'll be back soon. In the meantime we need to organize a search party. Go to the Crazy Horse and get Boomer and Jason and Jed Harely. I'll round up Cletus and the Anderson brothers and meet you at your place in, say, fifteen minutes.''

Clayt nodded once, then headed for the door. Wyatt wasn't far behind.

"Wait for me," Lisa called. Raising her chin a notch at the obvious question in Wyatt's eyes, she added, ''The sooner we get going, the sooner we'll find her.''

"We?" he asked.

She pushed her hair behind her shoulders and said, ''It just so happens that I know more about running away than anybody in Jasper Gulch. But just because I'd like to help you find Haley doesn't mean I've changed my mind about leaving town.''

Whatever glimmer of hope Wyatt had been harboring was extinguished by the look in her eyes. She'd made up her mind. Some of the people of Jasper Gulch had treated her horribly. And she was going to leave. He couldn't blame her for wanting to start over someplace else, could he? The hell he couldn't.

Cramming his hat on his head, he strode to his truck where he opened the door for her, the tilt of his head daring her to make something of it. It was very diplomatic of her to lower her gaze, and also very, very wise.

He slammed the door with an uncharacteristic show of impatience. Climbing into the driver's seat, he shoved the gearshift into First and headed for his grandfather's house beyond the outskirts of town.

The men who were huddled around the small fire looked up when Wyatt, Luke and Clayt rode in at a full gallop. Their expressions must have been extremely telling, because one look at their faces and the men turned back to the crackling flames.

Wyatt dismounted near the fence surrounding the corral, the Carson brothers following suit. ''Still nothin', eh, boys?'' Cletus asked, the tip of a smelly cigar glowing red in the darkness.

Clayt and Luke each hiked one foot onto a makeshift bench and shook their heads. Wyatt stood back a foot or two, surveying the scene. It was shortly after five in the morning and dark as night. The horses neighed softly, searching for tufts of green grass. Bits and pieces of conversation carried to his ears from the men by the fire, and every now and then tiny sparks rose on curls of smoke, only to blink out seconds later.

A half dozen men had begun the search last night. As the hours had slowly crept by, two dozen more men and women had shown up with spotlights and flashlights, lanterns and food. Once again the citizens of Jasper Gulch had rallied around one of their own. And in the midst of it all, Lisa had poured coffee and fixed plates of food for people who'd made her feel anything but welcome in their town. It made Wyatt so damn proud and so damn mad he wanted to shout it at the top of his lungs and demand an apology from each and every person in town.

Thunder rumbled in the distance, sending a sense of dread through everyone who heard. ''It's going to rain,'' Clayt said.

''Maybe,'' Cletus answered. ''Maybe not.''

''Haley's probably cold.''

''The sun will be up soon,'' Wyatt said. ''She'll warm up then.''

Clayt Carson was normally a man of few words, but the stress of the long night had taken a toll on him, making it impossible to hold everything inside. ''I talked to Boomer a couple of hours ago. He said the general consensus around here is that Haley ran away to find her mother. They think she might be long gone by now.''

''I highly doubt that, Clayt,'' Luke said, trying to reassure his brother. ''I think that deep down Haley knows her mother doesn't want her.''

"Yeah. Victoria never won any Mother of the Year awards. But if Haley didn't go to find her, she must have left because of what Isabell said."

Wyatt, Luke and Cletus muttered the same succinct cussword under their breath.

"What if I don't find her?"

"We'll find her," Wyatt said. And he meant it. "In the meantime she has a blanket and food and something to drink."

"Wyatt's right," Luke said. "I wouldn't be at all surprised if she comes walking back all by herself."

"I don't know anymore," Clayt said, thinking out loud. "I wouldn't have been so worried a month ago. Back then I believed that the biggest crimes in Jasper Gulch were jaywalking and gossip, and maybe the ugly color of orange Bonnie Trumble painted the front of the Clip & Curl. Now, I know that isn't so. Somebody stole Lisa Markman's car, and somewhere in Jasper Gulch is a person who's responsible for stealing women's underwear. What kind of a pervert would do that? And what would someone like that do to a nine-year-old girl?"

"Now don'choo go jumpin' to conclusions and lettin' your imagination run wild," Cletus declared. "There's a perfectly logical explanation for Lisa's missin' car, and we don't know that the person who took those bloomers is a pervert. I think Luke's right. I wouldn't be a bit surprised if Haley came walkin' back all by herself. But remember. That li'l girl's a female and a Carson. You put those two things together and you get stubborn with a capital S, and more spunk than even she knows what to do with."

Cletus's statement should have been comforting, but something about it left Wyatt feeling unsettled. Before he could put his finger on what it was, his gaze strayed to the lighted window in the kitchen where Lisa was ladling something into bowls for the Anderson brothers. He had no idea what Neil Anderson said, but Wyatt had seen Lisa toss her hair behind her shoulders and jut out one hip in precisely that way a hundred times. She'd always been sultry and warm and more than a little brash. That woman was a unique mixture of spunk and goodness, but when God had handed out obstinacy, Lisa Markman must have been the first in line. Not that there was a law against being stubborn. Hell, if there were, everyone on the planet would be behind bars.

Try as he might, Wyatt couldn't make sense of the way some of the people had treated her. What reason could Isabell Pruitt possibly have for boycotting Lisa's store? And why would anybody steal her, er, underpants and bras?

He didn't know how things had gotten so out of control. Two months ago the grass had been drying up on the plains, and he'd begun to think he would never meet the kind of woman he wanted to spend the rest of his life with. Now, more rain was forecast, and the woman he loved could very well slip through his fingers.

"Come on, boys," Cletus mumbled. "Let's go in the house and see what Lisa and Mel and Jillian have been cookin'."

Pulling a face, Luke said, "If Jillian cooked it, it probably isn't fit for man or beast. My future bride can't boil water."

"Then why are you marrying her?" Clayt asked quietly.

"Because," Luke said, staring at the red-haired woman on the other side of the kitchen window, "there are ways to a man's heart that have nothing to do with his stomach."

Cletus snapped a suspender and raised one craggy brow.

"It isn't what you're thinking," Luke declared. "At least it isn't *only* what you're thinking. Jillian makes me laugh, and she makes me think. She's going to be a wonderful teacher someday, and a wonderful mother."

Clayt dragged his hat off his head and raked his fingers through his hair. "Haley could use a woman like that."

Staring toward the house, Cletus said, "Now ain't hardly the time, Clayton, but after we find Haley, I've got a little proposition for you. We'll head back out to look for Haley as soon as the sun comes up. By George, we'll comb every last inch of these plains if we have to. But first, let's eat. I'm hungry as a horse."

One of the horses snorted indignantly. Wyatt, Clayt and Luke looked at one another. If they hadn't been so tired, and if the situation hadn't been so serious, they probably would have grinned.

At 7:00 a.m. Haley still hadn't been found. Since Wyatt had to check in at the office, Lisa had decided to catch a ride with him, thereby making room for the new batch of volunteers gathering in Clayt's kitchen.

She leaned her head against the side window, exhausted. Glancing at her little house with its tiny porch and old-fashioned swing, she said, "Thanks for the lift, Wyatt. Again."

"No problem."

She'd never known Wyatt to be a man of so few words. His hat was lying on the seat between them, his hair indented slightly where the dusty Stetson had sat most of the night. His chin was covered with twenty-four hours' worth of whisker stubble; his clothes bore the telltale signs of twenty-four hours' worth of wear and tear.

She'd once thought he looked like the kind of lawman who spent most of his time rescuing kittens out of trees. Last night she'd seen him in action, and she would never think of him that way again. The people of Jasper Gulch respected him. When he spoke, they listened; when he organized, they proceeded.

She'd found him watching her several times throughout the night and had lost track of how many times she'd wanted to go to him, to place her hand on his cheek and bring out his smile. Once she almost gave in to the need to touch him, but before she'd made it halfway across the room, she'd overheard Boomer and Jason singing his praises as a sheriff. So, instead of reaching out to him, she'd served him piping-hot chili and steaming coffee.

If she'd had any doubts about what she should do, she didn't anymore. Wyatt belonged here. And she didn't. Soon everything would be back to normal. Haley would be found, Wyatt would continue to be the sheriff of Jones County, and she'd find a way to earn a living someplace else. Maybe she'd start her catering business up again in Madison. Cori and Allison and Ivy were there, so she wouldn't be completely alone. But she would always be lonely.

The click of Wyatt's door brought her out of her musings. Pushing her own door open, she said, "I can find my own way in, Wyatt."

He looked at her, lifting his eyebrows in that argumentive way she was coming to recognize. They both got out and slowly made their way to her front door. A board on one of the steps creaked beneath their weight. Glancing down, she said, "I'll have to get a hammer and fix that before I leave."

Wyatt peered down at her. "You know how to pound nails?"

"Are you kidding?" she asked, her old haughtiness returning for a moment or two. "I spent two years helping Cori and Ivy turn an old house into a Victorian bed-and-breakfast inn."

"You can wait tables, run a store, pound nails and cook up a storm. Tell me, Leese, is there anything you can't do?"

Her eyelashes cast shadows on her cheeks every time she blinked. Her expression darkened and her voice shook slightly as she said, "There's one thing I can't do. I can't change my past."

Other than the wind howling through the eaves and the boy delivering the morning paper down the block, the street was utterly quiet. Keeping his voice low, he asked, "Would you change the past if you could?"

She looked up at him and slowly shook her head.

Wyatt stood perfectly still, but inside, his breathing deepened, his heart rate accelerated, and his emotions stirred. Lisa hadn't had a storybook childhood. Hell, he should get a prize for the world's biggest understatement. Yet she wouldn't change it. Her past had shaped her into the woman she was today, the woman he loved. Wyatt wouldn't change that, either.

Desire pulsed through him with so much force he was tempted to swing her into his arms and carry her inside. He'd been harboring some pretty incredible fantasies about the pleasure he'd bring her. Since he couldn't do what he wanted to do, he leaned forward slightly and did the next best thing. He whispered a kiss along her cheek, then moved on to her mouth. If he lingered a little longer than he'd intended, he couldn't help it. He was only a man, after all.

Leaving her to make whatever she chose of his kiss, he raised his face from hers, turned on his heel and left.

Wyatt leaned back in his chair and propped his feet on his desk. Something had been nagging him since the wee hours of the morning, and although the shower he'd taken after dropping Lisa off earlier had cleared his head, he couldn't seem to put his finger on what was bothering him.

He clasped his hands behind his head and stared up at the ceiling. It was almost eleven a.m., and Haley still hadn't been found. She'd left everything she loved behind, and there had been no sign of a struggle. Half the town had turned out to search this morning, and every single person had a two-bit theory as to where she'd gone and why. His grandfather always said that one thing small-town people had was strong opinions, and Cletus had a tendency to be right.

Wyatt straightened. Something his grandfather had said in the middle of the night flashed through his mind.

Now don'choo go jumpin' to conclusions, Cletus had declared out by the fence at the Carson ranch. *There's a perfectly logical explanation for Lisa's missin' car, and we don't know that the person who took those bloomers is a pervert. I think Luke's right. I wouldn't be a bit surprised if Haley came walkin' back all by herself.*

Wyatt let his feet drop to the floor and slowly stood. He didn't believe his grandfather had anything to do with Haley's disappearance. Everybody in town knew that Cletus wasn't above cheating in poker now and then, and he had been caught bending the rules from time to time. But he was a kind, decent man who would never willingly cause Clayt this kind of pain and worry.

There's a perfectly logical explanation for Lisa's missin' car, he'd said.

Not *there might be,* or *there probably was,* or *maybe.* He'd said there *is.*

The two anonymous tips Wyatt had received over the telephone concerning Lisa's stolen car played through his head. Although there had been something familiar about the voice, the connection had been so poor he hadn't been able to place it. Try as he might, he couldn't seem to keep two and two from making four. Without stopping to analyze his reasoning or his judgment, he strode straight to his cruiser, and headed south out of town.

Wyatt pulled the car to a stop so abruptly the tires slid in the loose gravel in the driveway. He rounded the hood, making a beeline for the house. "Cletus!" he called, checking every room.

A cup of cold coffee sat in the dish drainer, and a pair of overalls hung by the back door, but his grandfather was nowhere in sight. Hurrying outside again, Wyatt stood on the stoop and looked around. "Granddad?" he called loudly.

With a sense of dread dogging his steps, he headed straight for the barn. It took a moment for his eyes to adjust to the dim interior, but it didn't take long to recognize the red car with Wisconsin license plates sitting in the middle of the dirt floor.

For a moment all he could do was stare at the dust floating on the ray of light slanting through a crack in the wall. Oh, no. Granddad. Not you.

How in the hell was he going to arrest his own grandfather?

Wyatt had a pretty good idea why Cletus had taken the car. Oh, the old man probably didn't consider what he'd done a felony. He'd probably done it for the same reason he'd tossed that coin that day in Wyatt's office. To get him and Lisa together.

The new friends Cletus made in prison would probably have a dang field day with his story.

He wondered what Lisa would say about it.

Lisa.

Maybe he could salvage something here. After all, there wasn't really a car thief in these parts. Wyatt cringed. Who was he trying to kid? No matter *why* Cletus had done it, the fact of the matter was he'd done it.

All Wyatt could do now was find Lisa and explain what he'd found. Who knows. Maybe they could find a way around this.

And maybe his grandfather wouldn't go to jail.

And maybe they'd find Haley before it rained.

And maybe Lisa wouldn't leave Jasper Gulch.

Aw, hell. That was an awful lot of *maybes* for Wyatt's peace of mind.

Chapter Eleven

Lisa turned when the bell sounded over the door and found Wyatt looking at her from the doorway, an unreadable expression on his face. "Can you lock up the store and come with me?"

She stared at him, trying to understand what had put the clipped tone in his voice and the pensive shadows in his eyes. It wasn't that she believed he didn't have plenty to worry about. Things had been going from bad to worse for days. If his expression was an accurate indication, they'd just gone from worse to horrible.

"Where are we going?" she asked, reaching for her purse and her keys.

"To my grandfather's place," he said, then turned on his heel.

There wasn't much she could do except follow him out to the cruiser that was parked out front. Before she could ask if something new had taken place, Opal and Louetta Graham came out of the Clip & Curl and headed their way. Opal raised her double chin, and Louetta clutched her oversize purse close to her chest as she passed, but neither of them met her eyes. Watching them walk down the sidewalk and disappear inside the diner, Lisa felt a pang of sadness at the loss of a friend.

"Why are we going to Cletus's place?" she asked quietly.

"There's something I have to tell you. And I think the only way to do that is to show you."

She quirked one eyebrow. "If this is your version of 'I'll show you mine if you show me yours,' you're in big trouble, Wyatt McCully."

Wyatt looked at her over the top of the car, every male hormone in his body surging to life. Even dog tired and downtrodden, Lisa was sultry and warm and more than a little brash. Reminding himself to breathe, he said, "Believe me. This is on the up-and-up. For once in my life, I wish it weren't."

They drove to his grandfather's house in silence. Once there, Wyatt led the way into the old weathered barn. Inside, he blinked, refocused, then blinked again. Striding to the center of the dirt floor, he turned in a complete circle.

"What was it you wanted to show me?" Lisa asked from the doorway.

Wyatt glanced over his shoulder and clamped his mouth shut. Lisa had asked a perfectly logical question. Problem was, he didn't know what to say. Except for cobwebs and dust and a couple of old saddles, the barn was empty.

Relying on instinct alone, he strode to the big door and slowly pushed it open to get more light. He squatted down to examine the tire tracks in the loose dirt. Straightening, he measured the boot print against his own. It matched the print he'd found in Lisa's driveway the morning her car had been stolen. What was going on?

"Wyatt?"

He turned to face her and slowly shook his head. "Your car was here an hour ago."

"My car?"

He dragged his hat off his head only to cram it back on moments later. "I don't know what's going on, but I'm going to find out if it's the last thing I ever do. First, I have to find Cletus."

"You think your grandfather had something to do with my missing car?" she asked incredulously.

Oh, he thought his grandfather had something to do with it all right. In fact, he'd bet his badge that his grandfather was in it up to his ears.

The trip back into town was as quiet as the trip out to Cletus's place had been. Finding the bench in front of the post office empty, Wyatt decided to try his luck in the diner. He and Lisa strode in just as Opal and Louetta were coming out. Once again Louetta was clutching her oversize purse close to her chest. Once again she wouldn't meet Lisa's eyes, and once again Lisa felt a pang of loss.

"I don't understand it," she said quietly. "I thought Louetta and I were friends. We had some wonderful heart-to-heart talks every day when she came into the store."

Wyatt was scanning the diner's interior, but he must have been listening with one ear, because he said, "Louetta Graham came into the store every day?"

Lisa nodded. "Just like clockwork."

"What did she buy?"

"She didn't *buy* anything. She just browsed. Actually, she spent a lot of her time looking at the lingerie."

Lisa stopped, and Wyatt's gaze swung to hers. "Lingerie?" they mouthed at the same time.

They hurried back out to the street, but Opal and Louetta were nowhere in sight. "I think I should pay Louetta a little visit," Wyatt said.

They arrived on the Graham doorstep within minutes. "Is Louetta here, Opal?" Wyatt asked the instant the stout woman answered his knock.

Patting her gray bun, Opal said, "Why, no, dear, she isn't, but I'm sure she'll be sorry she missed you."

Lisa almost smiled at Wyatt's masculine snort. "Do you know where she is?" he asked.

"Why, I think she was going to return that new purse she bought at the five-and-dime. I don't understand why she purchased such a monstrosity in the first place. It's so out of character for her."

Lisa stood to the side, being as unobtrusive as possible. When Wyatt finally extricated himself from Opal's clutches, they both hurried back to the car. Out of hearing distance of Opal, she said, "I don't think you'll find Louetta at the dime store, Wyatt."

"You don't?"

She shook her head. "I have a feeling she's at 203 Elm Street."

"That's your address."

"I know. Let's go."

Wyatt pulled to a stop at the curb in front of Lisa's house and cut the engine. Being extra careful to close her door without making a sound, she gestured to the side yard. They crept around the house like detectives in a B-rated movie. Coming to a stop near a bed of dried-up poppies, they peered around the corner, then froze at the sight of Louetta Graham clipping bits of satin and lace to the clothesline.

Some sixth sense must have alerted Louetta to their presence. She tensed and slowly turned around. Looking as if she could faint at any moment, she met Lisa's gaze.

"Hi," Lisa said, stepping carefully out into the open.

Louetta dropped the last item to the ground and brought her hands up to her face. "I'm so sorry," she cried. "I didn't mean to steal your things. I only wanted to borrow them, so I'd know how it feels to be sensuous and beautiful instead of plain and mousy. I didn't try on the panties. I just held them up for effect, but I tried on the bras. And…''

Her voice faded as if she were running out of steam, out of breath and out of courage.

Slowly walking closer, Lisa asked, ''Did you like them, Louetta?''

The other woman nodded, her face flaming. ''I thought I'd be able to put everything back without you ever knowing. But you came home early that day, and then everything went sort of crazy.''

Bit by bit, things began to make sense. Lisa remembered how longingly Louetta had gazed at the pretty undergarments in the store. Now that she thought about it, she *had* almost run headlong into her the day she'd discovered her lingerie was missing. Lisa had been so intent upon telling Wyatt about the stolen items, she hadn't stopped to talk to Louetta. If she had, all of this might have been avoided.

''Are you going to arrest me, Wyatt?''

''Oh, my poor baby!''

Lisa, Wyatt and Louetta all turned to find Opal Graham standing near the house, her double chin shaking, her face white as a sheet. ''Merciful heavens! I knew something was bothering Louetta at lunch. Are you going to arrest my Louetta, Wyatt?'' she implored.

Lisa waltzed to the clothesline where she promptly unfastened the bras and panties. Reaching for the oversize purse, she said, ''I don't see why Wyatt would arrest Louetta for accepting a gift from a friend, do you?''

With that, she placed the bras and panties in the big purse. Handing it to Louetta, she said, her voice soft so only Louetta could hear, ''I think you're very brave. And with just a few changes, like wearing your hair down and buying clothes that suit you, your natural beauty will be evident for everyone to see.''

Louetta brushed a tear from her flaming cheek.

''I'll never breathe a word of this to anybody,'' Lisa

said gently. "If you'd like to come into the store tomorrow, I'll help you choose clothes that suit you. After all, I always knew you had a figure underneath those prim and proper blouses."

Lisa's wink came as no surprise to Wyatt, but it made Opal gasp. Recovering, the other woman nodded stiffly and said, "Thank you, Ms. Markman."

"Please," Lisa said with a tired smile. "My friends call me Lisa."

"Yes, yes, well, thank you, er, um, thank you." All stiff dignity and starched cotton, Opal hooked her arm through Louetta's and strode away.

Within seconds Wyatt and Lisa were alone. Facing her across the tiny expanse of her backyard, he said, "You're quite a woman, Lisa Markman."

"Aren't I, though?"

She laughed, the sound sneaking into his chest, dropping to the pit of his stomach and slowly pulsing lower. They were both in dire need of a good night's sleep, but in that instant, Wyatt felt far from tired. He strolled forward, coming to a stop directly in front of her.

He wanted to ask her if she was having second thoughts about leaving, but he didn't trust her answer. Lisa may have been stubborn, but he'd go toe-to-toe with her any day. And if she thought he was going to make it easy for her to leave, she could think again.

"One down, two to go?" she asked.

He didn't know how she did it, how she exuded so much sass and vitality with a simple lift of her chin and quirk of her brow. If she had this much spunk in the light of day, he could only imagine what she'd be like in the dark. The very idea fueled his longing.

He slid his fingers into her hair, tipping her face up as he lowered his mouth to hers. Something thudded to the ground beside them, and the kiss ended before it began. Lisa bent down to retrieve the neighbor children's ball, and

Wyatt cussed under his breath. Just once he'd like to kiss her without being interrupted, without being watched and without being on duty or having someplace he had to go. Just once he'd like to have all night. No, that wasn't true. Once would never be enough. He wanted to have all night for the rest of his life.

Taking her hand, he drew her with him around the shaded side of her house. They emerged from the shadows, only to find Opal waiting for them.

She clutched her wicker purse in both hands and took a tentative step toward Lisa. Head held stiffly, she said, "Louetta has gone home, but there's something I simply must say."

"Yes?" Lisa asked.

Opal's double chin shook ever so much as she said, "I know I already thanked you for treating my daughter with so much care, but I want to thank you again. I'm not sure I could have been half as gracious."

Wyatt almost croaked—of course the old biddy wouldn't have been half as gracious—but he glanced at Lisa, and the sound never made it out of his mouth. Her eyes appeared huge and were glazed with unshed tears.

Opal swallowed convulsively. Although her voice sounded forced, she said, "I raised her on my own, you know, ever since my Frank died. Anyway, I'd like to take this opportunity to invite you to the next Ladies Aid Society meeting. I wouldn't blame you for holding a grudge, but I hope you'll consider joining. We really do strive to better the community."

For the first time in Wyatt's life, he was tempted to kiss the old bat. On second thought, he would rather kiss Lisa. He waited for Opal to get in her car and pull away, then reached for Lisa's hand. Two boys rode past on bicycles, and a curtain fluttered in a window across the street. Clenching his jaw, he strode to the cruiser and opened her door. He was going to kiss her, but, by God, it wouldn't be in front of a dozen curious eyes.

Lisa felt as if she were floating, and she knew it was more than fatigue, and more than the first tentative steps Opal had taken to welcome her to this town. The sense of giddiness filling her was a result of the look deep in Wyatt's eyes, and the knowledge that she'd put it there.

Everything had changed today. Her reason for leaving and her reason to stay. Her heart beat with the pulse of the music playing over the radio. Strangely, it didn't stop when Wyatt pulled into his driveway and turned the key.

He pulled her with him out his side of the car, then wrapped his arms around her as if he'd waited as long as he could. His mouth covered hers, raw with need and so eager a knot rose to her throat. She twined her hands around his back, savoring the sheer size and strength of the man in her arms.

"Looky who I found campin' out in your shed, Wyatt."

Lisa and Wyatt jerked apart, their gazes swinging to an old shed near the back of his property. Cletus started toward them, Haley's small hand clasped tightly in his gnarled old fingers.

"Haley," Lisa exclaimed, hurrying toward the child. "Are you all right?"

The girl nodded solemnly. Although there were cobwebs in her hair and dirt smudges on nearly every inch of her, she appeared perfectly healthy. "I'm in trouble again, aren't I?"

Going down on one knee close to her, Wyatt said, "Your father has been worried sick. Why did you run away?"

Haley's eyes went to the toe of her shoe, and in a voice smaller than she was, she said, "I dunno. Sometimes I do stuff. I don't know why."

Suddenly remembering a certain car he'd found parked in a certain barn, Wyatt straightened and leveled a shrewd look at his grandfather. "Is there anything you'd like to get off your chest, Granddad?"

The old coot snapped one suspender and shrugged, as innocent as could be. "I cain't say that there is. It's quite a coincidence that I decided to look for Haley here, don'choo think? Quite a coincidence, indeed."

Wyatt lowered his chin and narrowed his eyes.

With a wink every bit as coy as Lisa's, Cletus said, "Things have a way of workin' out, don't they, boy?"

"Granddad," Wyatt said ominously.

Drawing Haley with him, Cletus said, "Since I don't wanna make poor Clayton worry a minute longer, I think I'll jist take Haley on home."

Lisa couldn't help smiling as she watched the two wily characters amble away, one, a skinny-legged little girl, the other a bandy-legged old cowboy. Turning to face Wyatt, she whispered, "One by one the mysteries are being solved. And one by one my dreams are coming true."

"Does that mean you've changed your mind about leaving?"

Before she could do more than nod, he swung her off her feet and spun her in a circle. Casting him a wry grin, she said, "Are you sure about this, Wyatt? My reputation will never be lily-white, and yours is still as sterling as your—"

A flash of color inside the shed drew her gaze. What the—

"Leese, where are you going?"

She didn't stop to answer until she'd walked through the small door. It was cool and dark inside the shed, but enough light shone through the window to guide Lisa's steps. Taking a quick, sharp breath, she ran her hand over her car's smooth red fender. She started at the sound of footsteps behind her, but she didn't turn around.

"That's your car," Wyatt declared.

"Yes, I know."

"What's it doing here?"

"That's what I was about to ask you."

Wyatt McCully had never stuttered in his life, but staring at the Wisconsin license plate on the back of Lisa's car, even his thoughts were coming in choppy bits and pieces. "Leese, I know how this must look. I mean, I know it looks bad...but I'd never...you don't really think I..."

"Why, Wyatt McCully," she said huskily, "it looks as if we might be more alike than I realized."

"Leese, I can explain."

She sashayed closer, her eyes trained on his mouth, her look of dismay turning warm and sultry. The next thing he knew, she was hurtling herself at him. Doing the only thing a sane, hot-blooded man could do, he wrapped his arms around her and accepted her kiss, returning it with all the passion he'd been trying to control for so long.

His hands slid down her back, kneading her soft flesh. He pulled her against his body, answering the sound she made deep in her throat with a low groan of his own. When the kiss finally ended, she whispered, "What was it you wanted to explain?"

Staring at the sass in her brown eyes, his disbelief turned into a welcome surge of excitement and an indefinable feeling of rightness. Grinning wickedly, he reached for her hand. "I'll tell you later. Right now, there's something I've been aching to do."

Outside, he held her gaze, and slowly went down on one knee. Her hair appeared even darker against the gray sky, and her eyes were trained on his. She was wearing a dress he'd seen before in colors of muted grays and blues and lavenders that ruffled in the breeze. It was a dress made for a lady. For her.

"Will you marry me, Leese?" he said, his voice catching on her name.

Lisa's throat tightened, the tears in her eyes somehow intensifying the tenderness and the passion glittering in

Wyatt's golden brown eyes. If she lived to be a hundred, she'd never forget the way he looked at that moment, all cowboy brawn and masculine longing. He was exactly the kind of man she'd been looking for, exactly the kind of man she thought she'd never find.

As one tear slowly trailed down her cheek, she took a shuddering breath. "Oh, Wyatt."

"I love you, you know."

She half laughed and half cried at that, but there was nothing funny or sad about the depth of emotion she felt for this man. "And I love you."

Adrenaline surged through Wyatt, his heart pumped faster, and he could feel the heat under his skin. He straightened and quietly said, "I'm waiting for your answer. Will you marry me?"

Wyatt caught a glimpse of her irreverent wink and impish smile moments before she reached with both hands and whisked his hat off his head, sending it sailing to the grass behind him. Her laughter filled the quiet afternoon like a song; marvelous, catching. Drawing his face close, she whispered, "It's either marry you. Or arrest you."

He closed his eyes at the first brush of her lips against his, thinking that he was going to be her prisoner either way.

Sprinkles pattered down from the clouds, seeping into Lisa's hair and dampening her skin. She said a prayer of thanks for the chance to know and love this man with the sterling badge and bad-boy smile.

They kissed for a long time, out in the open in Wyatt's side yard. Many a passerby slowed down as they passed, and many a curtain fluttered behind watchful eyes. More than one woman wondered if Lisa planned to carry the style of dress she was wearing in her store. The phone lines were already buzzing with news of Haley Carson's return, and folks were speculating that a double wedding was just around the corner, the first in the history of Jasper Gulch.

"We can announce our engagement at the barbecue tomorrow," Wyatt said.

Lisa glanced at the street where a car was creeping by and at the window next door where she was pretty sure a curtain was fluttering. Smiling, she said, "I have a feeling this will be old news by then."

"Darn gossips, anyway," Wyatt sputtered, scooping up his hat.

With a haughty lift of her chin, she said, "I don't think you should talk about the people of *our* town that way, do you?"

Gazing at the most delightfully unpredictable woman in the world, Wyatt shook his head and slowly extended his hand. Smiling, she placed her hand in his. He grinned wickedly, raised his face to the clouds and let loose a yowling yee-ha! The best part of their lives, and the best part of forever, had just begun.

* * * * *

Miss Melody McCully is mighty tired of being
overlooked by the Jasper Gents, but she's about to
do something to change that. Don't miss the fun—
and romance—when Sandra Steffen's
BACHELOR GULCH *series continues with*
CLAYTON'S LAST CHANCE LADY,
available in October only from Silhouette Romance!

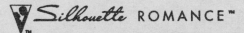

Take 4 bestselling love stories FREE

Plus get a FREE surprise gift!

Bestselling author

JOAN JOHNSTON

continues her wildly popular miniseries with an
all-new, longer-length novel

The Virgin Groom

HAWK'S WAY

One minute, Mac Macready was a living legend in
Texas—every kid's idol, every man's envy, every
woman's fantasy. The next, his fiancée dumped him,
his career was hanging in the balance and his future
was looking mighty uncertain. Then there was the
matter of his scandalous secret, which didn't stand a
chance of staying a secret. So would he succumb to
Jewel Whitelaw's shocking proposal—or take cold
showers for the rest of the long, hot summer...?

Available August 1997
wherever Silhouette books are sold.

Silhouette®

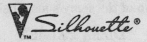

Share in the joy of yuletide romance with brand-new
stories by two of the genre's most beloved writers

DIANA PALMER

and

JOAN JOHNSTON

in

LONE STAR CHRISTMAS

Diana Palmer and Joan Johnston share their favorite
Christmas anecdotes and personal stories in this
special hardbound edition.

Diana Palmer delivers an irresistible spin-off of her
LONG, TALL TEXANS series and Joan Johnston crafts an
unforgettable new chapter to **HAWK'S WAY** in this wonderful
keepsake edition celebrating the holiday season. So
perfect for gift giving, you'll want one for yourself...and
one to give to a special friend!

Available in November at your favorite retail outlet!

Only from

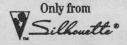

Silhouette®

You've been waiting for him all your life....
Now your Prince has finally arrived!

In fact, *three* handsome princes
are coming your way in

ROYAL WEDDINGS

A delightful new miniseries by **LISA KAYE LAUREL**
about three bachelor princes who find happily-ever-
after with three small-town women!

Coming in September 1997—THE PRINCE'S BRIDE

Crown Prince Erik Anders would do anything for his
country—even plan a pretend marriage to his lovely
castle caretaker. But could he convince the king, and
the rest of the world, that his proposal was real—before
his cool heart melted for his small-town "bride"?

Coming in November 1997—THE PRINCE'S BABY

Irresistible Prince Whit Anders was shocked to
discover that the summer romance he'd had years
ago had resulted in a very royal baby! Now that
pretty Drew Davis's secret was out, could her kiss
turn the sexy prince into a full-time dad?

**Look for prince number three in the exciting
conclusion to ROYAL WEDDINGS,
coming in 1998—only from**

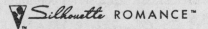

Silhouette ROMANCE™

**Beginning in September
from Silhouette Romance...**

a new miniseries by
Carolyn Zane

They're a passel of long, tall, swaggering cowboys who need tamin'...and the love of a good woman. So y'all come visit the brood over at the Brubaker ranch and discover how these rough and rugged brothers got themselves hog-tied and hitched to the marriage wagon.

The fun begins with
MISS PRIM'S UNTAMABLE COWBOY (9/97)

"No little Miss Prim is gonna tame me! I'm not about to settle down!"
   —Bru "nobody calls me Conway" Brubaker
"Wanna bet?"
   —Penelope Wainwright, a.k.a. Miss Prim

The romance continues in
HIS BROTHER'S INTENDED BRIDE (12/97)

"Never met a woman I couldn't have...then I met my brother's bride-to-be!"
   —Buck Brubaker, bachelor with a problem
"Wait till he finds out the wedding was never really on...."
   —the not-quite-so-engaged Holly Fergusson

**And look for Mac's story coming in early '98 as
THE BRUBAKER BRIDES series continues, only from**

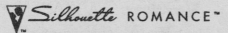